LONESOME RANGE

He had many names. He was the fastest gun in Texas, Colorado, or just about anywhere. When he was recognized, the challengers would come, guns would blaze and he'd ride away from yet another dead man. Then came the day where he'd killed one too many and the fastest gun had to swap his Colt for a sledge on the rockpile — for ten long years. But a chance for freedom came along, and he grabbed it with both hands . . .

Books by Tyler Hatch
in the Linford Western Library:

A LAND TO DIE FOR
BUCKSKIN GIRL
DEATHWATCH TRAIL
LONG SHOT
VIGILANTE MARSHAL
FIVE GRAVES WEST
BIG BAD RIVER
CHEYENNE GALLOWS
DEAD WHERE YOU STAND!
DURANGO GUNHAWK
KNIFE EDGE
WILDE COUNTRY
WILDCATS
RAWHIDE RANSOM
BRAZOS FUGITIVE
DEAD-END TRAIL

TYLER HATCH

LONESOME RANGE

Complete and Unabridged

LINFORD
Leicester

First published in Great Britain in 2011 by
Robert Hale Limited
London

First Linford Edition
published 2012
by arrangement with
Robert Hale Limited
London

The moral right of the author has been asserted

British Library CIP Data

Hatch, Tyler.
    Lonesome range. - - (Linford western library)
    1. Western stories.
    2. Large type books.
    I. Title II. Series
    823.9'2–dc23

    ISBN 978–1–4448–1165–0

Published by
F. A. Thorpe (Publishing)
Anstey, Leicestershire

Set by Words & Graphics Ltd.
Anstey, Leicestershire
Printed and bound in Great Britain by
T. J. International Ltd., Padstow, Cornwall

This book is printed on acid-free paper

1

Night Runner

Crossing the desert at night had been his best effort yet: it had put him many miles ahead of the searchers — and in a direction they wouldn't expect.

Too many had died in that desert over its long history: fugitives as well as travellers stayed away from it.

'Well, I got news for you, fellers — I made it!'

But it had taken a lot out of him, a hell of a lot, slogging through ankle-deep alkali and floundering up — and down! — those loose-sided dunes that seemed as high as mountains. The stars had been brilliant — he could still see a few as he lay on his back half-under a bush, letting his pounding heart settle and hoping the roaring of the blood in his ears would diminish quickly — and

1

they had guided him well. *He hoped so, anyway!*

It was pleasant here now, cool grey air just before sun-up. But he could use a long drink of water and some grub in his belly. For now, he had to try and sleep a little — *a little!* He couldn't afford to drift off into the deep, recuperative sleep his body needed. Not until he was well clear of the desert and deep into the ranges he knew must lie over that last rearing dune.

Even in his mind, the words began to slur and the vague vision blurred as he slid away into sleep . . .

His aching body wouldn't allow him to get comfortable, and it was only a fitful hour or so of tossing and turning before he awoke with a start — and, despite his fatigued mind, realized at once where he was.

Instinct took over and he rolled stiffly to hands and knees, involuntary groans and grunts escaping from scaled lips. Up on his feet he swayed, let the world settle to a more-or-less even keel, then staggered away towards the huge sandhill. Halfway there, reddened eyes gritty and blurring his vision, he saw that he was almost at one end of the dune: it tapered steeply and he thought he glimpsed a flash of green 'way beyond — trees, some brush and a grassy meadow on the lower slopes of a mountain . . .

That was the way for him! Instead of going up and over — the sand looked very loose anyway, some sliding now in a rippling wave even as he watched. Trying to crawl up that would be impossible — he would be buried under tons of sand in minutes.

So, through the half-light that still prevailed, he stumbled his way along the edge of the dune, gratefully found solid ground, even sparse patches of grass under his worn boots: *how much longer would they last . . . ?*

His body and mind quickly adjusted to the same old semi-trance-like rhythm that had gotten him this far: he was used to the spinning of the world around him now, the swirl of blue sky, streaked by white or occasional grey clouds.

And sometimes the rush of hard ground coming up to meet him and slamming him into a world of spinning stars and flashes that quickly disappeared and left only blackness.

Suddenly, everything changed.

Only partly aware of what he was seeing, he heard the rush of a breeze through brush and tree tops; saw a sapling bend and wave, and, beyond the first scattered vegetation, there was green rising solidly against the sky, dark, verdant green — which meant water.

He would have to search for it, but he knew what signs to look for and . . .

Instead of dreaming about it, he stopped thinking and willed his tortured muscles to action, filling his mind with only one thing now — cool, clear water.

He laughed, maybe a little crazily: *cool? clear?*

Hell! He'd drink water from a muddy hoofprint — or from the Devil's boots — as long as he drank!

He staggered on, making little moaning sounds in the back of a throat that burned like the grey sands he had just left behind . . .

★   ★   ★

It was night again.

At first he didn't know where he was, but the knotted growling of his belly soon reminded him. He was starving and half-dead, lost in some lonesome range that could be nudging the back corner of Hell for all he knew.

He remembered now: he had found water after first sucking the muddy roots of some grass which had kept him going until he came across a piece of sludgy ground, beyond which was a creek a man could step across — if he had the energy.

Thirst slaked, he rested —

'God almighty!' he breathed looking

at the sky. He must've slept the day away!

And he was still undiscovered! Still free!

He might be half-starved, but he had water and that would keep him going. In amongst all this vegetation, he would be able to find something to eat — wild onions, mushrooms, even the bark of certain trees. He could even peel bark and make it into thin strips using his horny thumbnails, maybe catch a fish . . . there were worms in the moist soil here.

But first, he had to find out where he was, before he even considered holing up here.

The night was cool and he groped his way through the trees, crossing a hump, following the downslope, until he came to a rocky ledge that jutted out and gave him a restricted view of the valley that lay ahead. There was no real detail, but he sensed the open space, felt it urging him on towards it . . . *As if he had a choice!*

He dropped to one knee behind a rock as he suddenly glimpsed distant pinpoints of light: they could mean a cabin — *and people!*

He didn't need people right now. He still had a long way to go to clear this country, though he figured he must have crossed the County Line about a day-and-a-half back. Still kneeling, he stared at those unmoving pinpoints, decided they were from a cabin — so, what was his next move?

Settlers meant grub, and other things. Like — a horse! He jumped when, at that very moment, he heard a sound he recognized, not too close, but his ears were well-attuned to sounds of this nature by now.

It was a creaking, distinctive sound — the kind a loose corral post made when a horse within its confines rubbed against it to scratch its hide or slick down an itchy patch of sweat. Even as he strained to hear, there was a vague snort of pleasure, followed by the dull scrape of shuffling hoofs.

Enough to give him direction — and this far from the cabin it ought to be safe enough to steal a mount. Saddle and harness would be a bonus but likely there wasn't any riding gear stashed this far out from the homestead.

He slithered down the slope towards the sound, hit his head hard on a low branch and felt the skin split above his left eye. He ignored the flow of blood, wiped a grimy sleeve across, and slithered down several more yards.

Panting, straining to see, he made out the shape of a small corral: a horse gave a snort of alarm as it heard him, and another answered. *He would have a choice of mounts. 'Oh, Lady Luck, stay with me tonight!'*

Chuckling to himself, he made his way to the pen, saw there were three horses and, judging by the way they were behaving, only half-broke. So this would be the breaking-in corral, only it wasn't far enough away from the cabin to warrant setting up a proper camp where the wrangler would sleep out. He could easily ride back to the cabin for his meals and . . .

By now he was standing on the bottom rail, talking softly to the skittish horses. He wasn't quite ready to risk slipping between the rails until he saw just how friendly — or otherwise — these half-mustangs were.

And then he heard the gun hammer cock behind him and felt the gun muzzle bruise his already sore spine, ramming him hard, face first, against the lodgepole.

'Hold it, you thievin' son of a bitch!'

He lifted his hands quickly, stepping down off the rail. 'Take it easy, friend!' he rasped. 'I'm just looking.'

There was a brief chuckle. 'Reckon Bracken told you to do more'n that! Look, maybe, but then wreck the corral an' turn loose our *remuda,* more likely!'

'I dunno any Bracken, and I . . . '

The rifle muzzle jabbed brutally into his midriff and he doubled over, stumbling forward. His head rammed against the unseen gunman and sent him staggering. The gunman must have taken it for some kind of attack, for he swore, stepped in fast and slammed the rifle butt into the intruder's chest, followed-up with a back-swing that clipped his head and knocked him sprawling. He fell half-under the bottom corral rail and the horses in there, nervous, spooked by the harsh voices and sounds they couldn't recognize, stomped and surged around.

The man with the gun, sighed and almost reluctantly dragged the semi-conscious man out from under. He planted a heavy boot on the heaving chest, lifted his rifle and loosed-off three fast shots, flame stabbing into the night sky.

The noise brought him out of his daze. 'What the . . . ? I ain't . . .'

The boot clipped him under the jaw and he went away in a shower of stars for a little while. There were a lot of queer sounds inside his head and blurred scenes passed in front of or behind his throbbing eyes.

The rifleman stood above him, his head and shoulders moving across the stars as he muttered half aloud, obviously referring to whoever it was he had summoned with his rifle shots. 'Come on! Come on!'

The man on the ground tried to speak and the rifle rapped the back of his hand as he reached up. It hurt, and he knew the bones were bruised and suddenly, despite his fatigue, rage surged through him. He reached up, grabbed the rifle and yanked. But the man had a tight grip and though pulled slightly off balance, he kicked out and his boot thudded into already sorely punished ribs.

The intruder came up off the ground, faster than the gunman expected, but was unsteady on his feet. The guard swung the rifle, and clipped him on the head, knocking him to his knees. He brought up his own knee into the stubbled, filthy face and stretched the man out on the ground.

But if he thought that was an end to it, he was badly mistaken. A surprisingly strong hand gripped one ankle and yanked violently. The rifle clattered as it fell, its owner crashing heavily on to his back, his head rapping the ground hard. The fugitive was on top of him in a moment, hooking an elbow against his throat. As the guard choked and gagged, boney knuckles crunched his nose and flattened his lips against splintering teeth.

But that had been about all the energy the intruder had and he stayed on hands and knees, head hanging, gasping for breath. The other, hurt, bleeding, spitting, lurched up, boots thudding into the intruder's side, knocking him over, ripped at his shoulder, the worn heel just missing his ear and face. The guard lost his footing, put down a hand to steady himself, straightened again and kicked hard.

The semi-conscious intruder briefly felt the jarring agony against his head and then plummeted into blackness . . .

He didn't hear the two horsemen ride in, skidding their mounts, guns in hands.

'The hell's all the racket, Pres?' one rider demanded.

Pres, dabbing a kerchief to his smashed mouth, gestured with his recovered rifle to the prone shape at his feet.

'Caught him trying to wreck the corral and set loose the *remuda* — just as well you made me stay out here overnight, Yuma.'

'Who is he?'

'Never said but has to be one of Bracken's crew.'

The third man had dismounted and knelt beside the unconscious intruder, scraped a vesta alight across his gunbelt. In the flare he looked at the filthy, bloody face in front of him.

'No one I recognize. Don't even look like a cowpoke — wearin' rags, got a three, four-day's growth of stubble, stinks like a desert Injun — ' He looked up over his shoulder to his mounted companion. 'I reckon we got us a

13

fugitive of some kind here, Yuma.' He flicked his gaze to the rifleman. 'Mebbe a dead one, if Pres's runnin' true to form.'

The mounted man swore. 'Just what we need! Goddamn you, Pres! You and your short fuse!'

'He busted my teeth, for Chris'sakes!' His protest was muffled behind the bloody kerchief. 'I weren't standin' still for that!'

'He dies or he don't, he's still a goddamn problem.'

'I'll take him back to the dune an' slide a couple tons of sand over him, no one'll ever find him.'

'Till the first big sand storm and then he's uncovered! Is he still breathin', Blue?'

'I've heard leakin' bellows in a blacksmith's make less noise . . . I reckon he's a dyin' man, Yuma. Might's well start diggin' a grave.'

'Goddamn you, Pres!' Yuma gritted again. 'One way or another, someone's gonna come lookin' for this ranny. If it's law, an' I lose The Bench because of it — I'll kill you. Now you take that as gospel, then start diggin' the grave.'

2

Man in a Shroud

He was choking — well, not exactly, but sure as hell his lungs were starved for air.

There was a roughness against his face. He could barely move his head and when he did there were rasping sounds and his ears hurt against whatever was covering him. His hands were down at his sides but he had only limited movement. Whatever was encasing him was fairly tight all the way down his body: there was pressure over his feet and it was hard to move them, though he managed a little.

That damn Warden! Thought up some new kinda torture?

Dimly, he heard scraping sounds, an occasional metallic ring . . . a muffled voice cursing. Then, louder, startled,

'Judas Priest! I — I seen that shroud move!'

'Just keep diggin', Pres!'

'No! Gospel! His, his boots moved! He's still alive!'

'Goddammit, Pres, if you think this'll get you off the hook, just delayin' things, you got another . . .'

'*Yuma*! He's right! I — I just seen his head move!'

More swearing, hands tearing at the tarp covering him.

'C'mon! Get him outta that damn shroud before he smothers! *Use your knife, you blamed idiot*!'

The blade sliced through the cord that had been roughly sewn through the canvas. He heard the stitches popping one by one and he gasped, gagged, coughed as the first blast of cool night air found its way into his lungs.

'Jesus, feller! We almost buried you!' rasped Blue, pushing the canvas down over the shoulders. 'Help me drag him out, Pres!'

There was a small fire burning and

the man just back from the dead blinked as he saw the partly-dug grave. They propped him up against a rock and Blue handed him a half-full mug of coffee. He wrapped his hands about the metal, burning them a little but un-caring. *Coffee! Man, it was weeks since he'd had real coffee! That burnt-bread muck they served in the Pen would poison a horny-toad . . .*

A gnarled hand pulled the mug away from his lips and he looked into the face of the man called Yuma: weath-ered, middle-aged, spikey with pepper-and-salt stubble. His breath was sour with old tobacco and whatever he had eaten for supper. Stained teeth showed as he grinned briefly.

'Not too fast. How you feel?'

It took the injured man a minute or so to think about what had happened to him and he lifted one hand and touched his head where there was a large knot forming.

'Like I just come back from the dead.' His voice was raspy, strained. He cleared his throat, looked around at the trio. *Obvious cowmen — Yuma was in charge, that was clear enough, Blue must be the one with the shoulder-length black hair, and one slit nostril: looked like an old knife wound . . .*

That left Pres — the one who had jumped him and beat him with the rifle butt . . .

Looked ordinary enough, but a closer examination of the dark eyes discovered the meanness there — and he could vouch for that! In his twenties, not ugly, nor handsome, just with the dark-skinned work-a-day look of any cowpoke between here and El Paso. *The mouth was mean, too, now he looked more closely . . .*

'You're in a helluva mess, feller,' Yuma said abruptly. 'Clothes look like they come outta a Texas Twister.'

The man seemed to be drifting away, but shifted his shoulders and frowned. 'Wha . . . ? Oh, yeah. Lost my rig other side of the desert . . . '

'*Other* side of the desert?' echoed Pres disbelievingly. He snorted. 'You ain't sayin'

18

you *walked* across that desert!'

The man looked at him, sun-blurred eyes steady. 'Had no choice,' he rasped.

The three cowmen exchanged glances.

'Posse?' asked Blue shrewdly.

No response.

'Ain't many Injuns round these days out here but guess a bunch of renegades mighta give you some trouble . . . ?' Yuma suggested, but again got no reaction: the man's blank stare didn't change.

Then Pres snapped, 'What's your name?'

A name . . . ? What could he call himself . . . ? Or maybe now would be a good time to pass-out again . . .

He swayed violently, spilled the coffee and started toppling sideways. Blue leaned forward swiftly and tried to steady him but he was a dead weight and he lowered the man to the ground — none too gently. He didn't even grunt.

Blue looked up at Yuma. 'Maybe closer to bein' dead than we thought.' Even as he spoke, he slipped a hand inside the ragged shirt and pursed his lips. 'Heart's goin' — kinda crazy rhythm but — it's pumpin'.'

Pres spat. 'Convenient time to pass out.' He leaned closer to the battered man, lifted a hand as if he would back-swipe him across the face but caught the hard look Yuma threw him and lowered it without striking the unconscious man. But he leaned even closer to his ear as he asked, 'Will I finish diggin' his grave or not . . . ?'

He smirked, expecting some kind of reaction — but there was none at all. *The collapse had been a fake, but now had passed into true unconsciousness* . . . . Pres shrugged, sat back and began to roll a cigarette, looking at Yuma as he licked the edge of the paper. 'Your problem, Yuma.'

'Of your makin' . . . ' Yuma glanced at Blue. 'Any ideas, Blue?'

'Not me. You're the boss of this outfit. Whatever you decide is OK by me.'

Yuma gave him a hard stare, shifted his gaze to the prone intruder.

'Well — don't think he's one of

Bracken's men.'

'Hell, no,' Blue agreed. 'Not in that shape. I guess we're about due for someone from Bracken, but he'd send a man with a gun in each hand.'

Yuma continued to stare at the unmoving man on the ground. After a long minute, he mused aloud,

'S'pose he could've gotten into that mess by walkin' across the desert . . . '

Pres snorted. 'I've knowed ox-teams with full supplies couldn't make it — just dropped in their tracks, fodder for the vultures.'

'Ye-eah,' Blue said, slowly nodding. 'If he *did* cross the desert, walkin', or even *flyin*', he musta had a damn good reason — or, like he said, — no choice.'

'Sounds like he's on the dodge to me,' opined Pres, as he lit his cigarette. 'No account, anyway you look at it. Just makin' more problems for us.'

Yuma nodded slowly, frowning deeply, finally said,

'Wonder if anyone'd miss him if we did just bury him . . . ?'

★ ★ ★

'You're dumb, Yuma, but not that dumb. You musta known you'd be hearing something from me.'

'Well, yeah. Just didn't expect you to come in person, Luke.'

'See? You are dumb! You jump my line camp, kick my crew off, then come up with a claim to the land — and you think I won't handle it personally?'

'What's there to handle, Luke?' You got no claim to this land anymore.'

'I say I have, so it's mine! Goddamnit, my crew built the cabin you're livin' in!' A brief silence and then, bitterly. 'Damn you, Yuma — it was open range! Free to all!'

'Sure, but you just threw up a line camp, moved in a crew — but *didn't file on it*! That was your mistake, Luke . . . I *filed a claim to it*! That makes it legally mine, with whatever's on it between the boundaries — you wanna argue, you're up agin the Gov'ment! And they're on my side now.'

A brief silence during which Luke Bracken was obviously stewing. The six mounted men behind him held their rifles across their knees but no one yet made a hostile move.

'Well,' Bracken said finally, 'That remains to be seen, don't it?'

'Any time you're ready.' Yuma sounded supremely confident.

'Aw, you'd be surprised at how ready I am, Yuma — I mean, the cabin burns down, the miserable bit of stock you've moved in either stampedes outta here or gets burned up, 'cause the fire'd sweep through that brush and them stands of young trees like a tide comin' in. There'd be nothin' left then.'

Yuma laughed without mirth. 'Nothin' for you, neither — except a long term in the Pen!'

'Me? Hell, I wouldn't know anything about what caused your fire — or how come you and your two half-wit cow-hands came to be burned to death — died game, I s'pose, fightin' to save what they could — *tsk, tsk, tsk*! Town'd be in

23

mournin' for all of ten minutes.'

Yuma's voice didn't sound so confident now. 'You'd never get away with cold-blooded murder, Bracken! You're a big man hereabouts, but not that big.'

Bracken's voice was hard, cold and merciless now.

'Aw, I'm that big, Yuma! And about to prove it.' Leather creaked as he hipped in the saddle. 'Any of you boys happen to have a spare match on you . . . ?'

Inside the cabin, the man standing pressed against the wall beside the second front window decided he had heard enough.

It was time to act . . .

There was a lot of movement in the front yard by now. Pres Barnes had been seemingly lounging by the well and now reached down for the rifle he had laid on the ground behind the low stone wall. But one of the riders broke away from Bracken's group, spun his horse in sharply as Pres rose and rode him down. Pres's body was hurled back several feet and then rolled four times through the dust before bringing up against a post of the newly-built corral. He lay there winded, dazed, shaking his head in an effort to clear it.

Blue managed to get off a shot from the incomplete barn but another of Bracken's riders dropped a lariat over his shoulders and dragged him clear across the yard, to leave him half-choked with dust, gasping and dazed, clothes torn, only a few feet from Bracken's big white horse.

The rancher was a big man, and he lifted a hand like a shovel as Yuma started to reach for his gun: it had all happened so fast the rancher had only just now been able to make his move. Bracken palmed up his own Colt smoothly.

'Just leave it, Yuma. Rather they didn't find any bullets in you but I ain't all that fussy about it . . . '

'How fussy are you about 'em finding a charge of buckshot in *your* hide?'

Every man there froze, at least momentarily, eyes swivelling towards the west front corner of the cabin.

A man stood there holding a double-barrelled Greener shotgun — both hammers were cocked and the muzzles moved in tight arcs, covering Luke Bracken's group.

Yuma, Blue and the dazed Pres — now sitting up in the dust — stared in disbelief at the shotgunner: he was the man they had caught trying to steal one of their half-broken mustangs out at Pinchgut Bend. Yuma had relented and brought him back here, days ago, tending his hurts, though he hadn't showed any signs of true consciousness up to this morning: murmurings and unintelligible shouts, but — *now!*

He was wearing a faded range shirt and trousers that hung loosely on his tall frame. His feet were bare and he held that shotgun like he not only knew how to use it, but was ready to use it given even half a chance.

'Who the hell's this?' Bracken addressed the question to Yuma — who was even more surprised than the big rancher. But he recovered quickly.

'Aw — din' I tell you, Luke? Hired me an extra hand.'

'An' just who the hell is he?'

Bracken's voice ended on a querying note and the man with the Greener said, readily enough, 'Vern Clinton.'

Bracken curled his thick lips. 'Never heard of you. Just another no-'count drifter, huh? Well, you know what happened to the others, Yuma. Hey, feller, whatever Yuma promised you, forget it. He can't pay fightin' wages — I can, but I'd naturally want to see what I was hiring. So, you turn that Greener around to cover Yuma and his two-bit crew and mebbe we can talk business.'

The shotgun barrels didn't waver, remained pointing directly at Bracken.

'Only move I'm making with this gun is to pull the trigger — while it's aimed at you — unless you take your men and clear out.'

Bracken's big shoulders stiffened. His face was heavy, thick-lipped, and he had bushy eyebrows, a big nose and a

27

jutting jaw. A frightening man to most folk.

'Yuma tell you who I am?'

'Know who you are. Don't need a name. Seen a hundred like you over the years. Even killed a few.'

Bracken stiffened even more and some of his men moved restlessly in their saddles. One man licked his lips and swallowed audibly. He earned a withering glare from Luke Bracken.

'Hired gun, huh?' Bracken swivelled his gaze to Yuma — who was just as stiff with tension as the big rancher and his men. 'Well, well, just remember, Yuma, you made the first move — and I damn well won't forget it!'

'Go home and think about it, Bracken.' Clinton advised, emphasizing his words with a slight upward jerk of the Greener's muzzles.

Bracken reared back involuntarily, his coarse face immediately colouring at this sign of what he would see as a display of weakness. 'I'll remember you, mister!'

'I'll make sure you do.'

Bracken hesitated only a moment longer, then savagely wrenched round the head of his big white. Red streaks showed on the pale flanks as he raked with his spurs, bringing a squeal of protest from the horse as it lunged away.

His men followed, one by one, leery about turning their backs on the shotgun. But when Clinton fired it, he pointed the barrels skyward, discharging only the right one.

As the thunder slapped across the bench and broke against the slopes where Bracken and his crew were riding, Yuma pulled off his neckerchief and wiped his sweating face.

'Guess I owe you one — Clinton, is it?'

'It'll do.' The man using that name broke the shotgun and pulled out the smoking used cartridge, took another shell from his shirt pocket and pushed it home, snapping the gun closed. By that time, Pres Barnes and Blue McElroy had come up. Both seemed somewhat wary of Clinton.

'Kinda glad we never buried you after all,' Blue said.

'Me, too.'

'Was Yuma's idea,' Pres said reluctantly, but making it clear there was no way he was going to thank Clinton for saving his hide from a greater beating than he'd already taken, after being ridden-down.

Clinton took Yuma's right hand when the man offered it, gripped briefly.

'Half expected to wake up looking at the grass roots,' Clinton admitted quietly. 'Then I figured no dirt grave was as comfortable as the straw mattress I was lying on — I only pretended to pass out when you asked my name up on that bench, but I slipped off *all* the way — last thing I heard, was you wondering if any one'd miss me if you buried me.'

Yuma smiled crookedly. 'Well — would they?'

Soberly, Clinton shook his head. 'No one I can think of right-off, mebbe a gal if I put my mind to it ... Some shouting woke me and I found these clothes on a wallpeg near the bunk I was lying on, the shotgun hung above 'em — it was obvious someone'd took care of me: bandages or iodine on my cuts and grazes, I'd been shaved, a few knocks and bumps and blisters on my feet treated — how come? You practising to be a sawbones or something?'

Yuma looked embarrassed, then shrugged. 'Just got it into my head that maybe you *did* walk across that desert — and if so — well, I could sure use a man like that. In any case, figured you'd earned somethin' better'n the 'welcome' Pres gave you.'

Pres's jaw jutted as he looked at Clinton flatly. 'I was there to see no one bothered the *remuda* — I don't have time to talk when I see someone tryin' to steal one of our hosses.'

Clinton rubbed at his bandaged head. 'You ought to try, learn to ask a man what he's doing — and why — before you start in beatin' him with a rifle butt.' He rubbed his tender sides. 'Or kick his ribs in.'

'You heard me! I ain't much for talkin'.' *In other words — 'Take it or leave it — or . . . !'*

Clinton held out the Greener to Yuma. 'This is yours, I guess.'

The man took it and Blue looked sharply at Pres — just in time to see Clinton's fist crash against the man's jaw and drop the cowboy to the dust.

'What the hell you doin'?' Yuma demanded, stepping forward.

Clinton didn't look at him, just lifted a hand and pushed the shotgun to one side. 'Pres and me've got some squarin'-away to do. Don't try to stop it.'

'Hell, man, you've been three days a-bed!'

Clinton smiled crookedly, watching the dazed cowboy start groggily to his feet. 'Just about makes it even then — wouldn't want to hold too much advantage over Pres.'

That was all it needed — as Clinton knew.

Pres came roaring to his feet and without stopping to think, hurled himself at Clinton, fists already hammering the air near the man's face.

Clinton weaved but was too slow, his recent ordeal catching up with him. Pres grinned tightly, stepped in close, planted a boot between Clinton's bare feet and his arms pistoned as he pummelled the other's already bruised ribs. Clinton staggered back, sagging, and Pres yanked one boot to the side and scooped a leg out from under him. As Clinton went down in the dust, Pres swung the other boot at his head.

This time, Clinton moved fast enough — just. The boot rippled his hair, it went that close. Then he rolled in towards the eagerly advancing Pres, came up like he was spring-loaded. He moaned aloud as the top of his head connected with Pres' lantern jaw, staggered back as stars burst behind his eyes, trailing wakes of searing pain.

But although the blow had hurt him, it had hurt Pres more. The man was floundering, going down, putting out one hand to save his fall. Clinton stumbled in close enough to kick that hand away and Pres hit the ground with a grunt.

He rolled on to his back and Vern Clinton stomped on his midriff with his hard-skinned heel — almost as tough as old leather. Pres gagged and his upper body snapped upwards, arms clamping across his mid-section. Weaving, almost going down with fatigue, Clinton rammed a knee against the side of Barnes' head. Pres tumbled over, face bloody, red streaks stark against the sudden paleness of his face.

But, like a lot of bullies, Pres was tough. He swivelled his legs around in a wild sweep, hitting Clinton in the shin. That leg collapsed and Clinton danced awkwardly, trying to keep balance. Pres was up on one knee, launching himself, head down, aiming to drive like a battering-ram into the hurt man's belly.

Clinton, vision blurred, senses reeling, wrenched his body around and

Pres missed, but his shoulder caught him on the hip. Clinton lurched, fought for balance, and Pres swept on — towards the well.

Clinton took a long, wavering step after him, tripped him, and Pres' face skidded through the dirt and his head rammed the stone wall.

He went limp, but his chest heaved with desperate effort as he fought for breath, blood streaking his face.

Clinton, dander well and truly up, his recent ordeal forgotten as the adrenalin stampeded through his system, drew back his foot and lifted it above the bloody face: one savage, downward blow would pulp Pres' face, maybe kill him with splintered bones driving into his brain.

Yuma lunged forward, shouting. 'That's enough! Goddamnit, you don't want to kill him!'

'Who — says . . . ?' panted Clinton and suddenly whipped Yuma's Colt from the man's holster in a blur of speed that left Blue blinking.

But as the swaying Cliton took the pistol in both hands, hammer already cocked, the rancher swung up the shotgun and rammed the muzzle against Clinton's side.

'I said enough!'

Clinton stared at him, his eyes filled with a strange light — a *killing* light. But he suddenly frowned and lowered the gun hammer, letting the weapon fall.

He sat down heavily, wiped blood from his nostrils, the world reeling about him. Blue hurried towards him, steadying him against his legs.

'Listen — Vern — you stay on here, I'm your friend, OK?' A brief pause as he glanced at the tensed Yuma. 'I'd sure as hell hate to be your enemy!'

Vern Clinton smiled briefly, showing blood-smeared teeth before he passed out.

3

The Bench

Two more days in bed were more than Vern Clinton could stand.

'Or take lyin'-down,' he told himself with a wry smile.

The small hurt as stiff and swollen muscles were called into action reminded him of the fight — if that's what it was — with Pres Barnes. *He'd have to watch it: that old drive that insisted he square a debt — or a hurt — as quickly as possible, no matter what . . . Over the years it had gotten him into a lot of trouble — but maybe this time, just maybe . . .*

He had found himself a haven here, if he played his cards right — but he couldn't relax, being confined to the big open room of the cabin while the others went about their chores. Or, he had to add, feeling kind of ungrateful, having Yuma and Blue fuss over him, telling him to take things easy. He only had to mention in passing that he liked coffee with a shot of whiskey in it, and within minutes he had a steaming mug of the stuff thrust at him.

He learned quickly not to make such slips very often, but he still felt helpless when they ganged-up on him. He knew they had his welfare at heart, but there was no reason now for him to make out he needed their attentions.

He'd always had it rough and no doubt had knocked a year or two off his life-expectancy with that trek across the desert, but he needed to get mobile again. His whole life had been one on the move for one reason or another — the family following his father's restless urges for 'a change of scenery', losing a little freedom as well as cash with each place they abandoned — Pa had been an optimist, was always 'sure as a bullet flies straight' that his fortune lay just over the next hill — or was it the one after that . . . ?

But now and again, even a bullet deviated from its prescribed path and dropped or veered suddenly . . .

Soon they were too poor to move, even too poor to settle — Pa had to take jobs working someone else's land — and he, Wade, had to take work — in place of schooling — so as to earn enough to keep vittles on the table.

Eventually, sickness claimed first his mother, then his young sister. Pa went to pieces, sought his future now by looking at it through the distorted bottom of a whiskey bottle . . . Until the gambler he owed money to but couldn't pay sent a man to make an example of him to others. It was a savage beating and Pa had taken four days to die.

The only legacy young Wade had were the clothes he stood up in, and the old man's six-shooter. It was a cap-and-ball single-action Colt. He knew how to use it, had brought home many a bullet-mangled rabbit and other small game for food. He had even strapped on the gunbelt and practised drawing swiftly as he could for his own amusement. When he was satisfied with his speed, he set about drawing faster, and shooting more accurately. It took a long time, popping empty bottles and coffee can lids, and he had earned more than one cuff across the head from Pa for using up their stock of black powder and sheet lead for moulding bullets.

Twice he won Junior shooting competitions but that was OK with Pa, specially if it was a cash prize.

But, after seeing Pa buried in a pauper's grave, young Wade sat by his campfire outside of town and cleaned and oiled the gun — and thought about that gambler and the man who had beaten Pa to death: he was just fourteen years old. A boy — big for his age, long on guts — and a strong sense of right and wrong. He decided the gambler and his bully-boy were *wrong*.

So he met them head-on — went straight to the sleazy saloon, coughed in the fug of smoke and whiskey fumes, walked right up to the table where the gambler was busy shuffling cards — dealing from the bottom of the deck, Wade reckoned — and said in a voice that hadn't long broken from childhood into the sometimes comical bray of the fading youthful years:

'You had Garr beat my Pa to death — for a lousy seven bucks!'

All at the table looked up, a couple of the men smiling crookedly, one saying, 'Hey, watch out, Deuce! You got a feller here I swear wants to eat you!'

The gambler looked up, long face unamused. 'I'd give him a bellyache — Garr!' He called to a man standing in the shadows by the end of the bar. 'Get rid of him.'

Garr was a big man, but sloppy looking, and had a mean twist to his mouth. 'Always kicked myself for not punchin' you into a bloody pulp when I took care of your old man, kid — Aim to set that to rights — *now*!'

One card player started to object but

at a warning from the man beside him stayed silent. Garr reached for Wade but jumped back when he saw the kid was ready to go for his gun.

'Why, you sassy li'l bastard!'

Leisurely, Garr went for his own gun, maybe only meaning to whip the kid with it, but he never got a chance.

Wade's Colt blasted and Garr's smirking face disappeared behind a large splash of blood. His head jolted like his neck would snap and his body crashed across the card table, upsetting it. The men leaped up and then flung themselves away from any more gun-play — and there was some.

The startled gambler drew his hideaway gun from under his armpit but hadn't even got it lined-up when Wade shot him twice through the chest. He went down, coughing and gagging, choking in his own blood.

'I hope you take four days to die, too, you son of a bitch!'

And then the kid was gone and life and noise came back into the stunned saloon — except for Garr and the gambler . . .

* * *

Those killings had troubled Wade for a long time and he had put away the gun and found honest work. But there came other occasions when he saw, even in his tender years, that some of his troubles could only be settled one way.

With a gun.

He had used this reasoning for a long time — for years — not consciously following a gunfighter's way, which would have been so easy to do, but rarely hesitating to resort to his gun when he figured he had to.

Of course, he earned himself a reputation whether he wanted it or not, and the life he led became even more restless than when Pa had been dragging his family all over the country looking for his fortune . . .

Sometimes he had had to run and keep on running, because the Law, or enemies, or kin of men who had gone down under his gun pursued him relentlessly . . .

Like that most recent time — down on the Panhandle in a town called, of all things, Pearly Gates. No doubt some found the name appropriate, but he wasn't able to stay long enough to decide.

He had to run and keep on running — and he had ended up here — in this well-built line cabin, now Yuma Hardy's ranch house, a long, long way from the Panhandle.

He couldn't help but wonder if it was far enough.

★   ★   ★

The man calling himself Vern Clinton was sitting alone on the end of the bench at the rough eating table under a brush-roofed ramada. It was near the kitchen door and as he lifted his mug of coffee to drain it, Pres Barnes came up, leading his work-pony for the day.

He stopped several feet from the table, face tight, eyes narrowed. Clinton saw him, nodded, held up the mug.

'Blue makes good java.'

'You an' me ain't through yet.'

Clinton lowered the mug, gaze steady on Pres' still-bruised face. 'We are — far as I'm concerned.'

Pres swung aboard the work pony, settled heavily. As he dug in his spurs and the mount started away, he said flatly,

'Get yourself a gun!'

Clinton watched him ride away, took tobacco sack and papers from the pocket of the denim work shirt Yuma had given him and began to build a cigarette. He turned his head as Blue came to the kitchen door and tossed a pan of soapy water into the yard. He was looking after Pres, now disappearing into the brush where the bench rose into the slope of the mountain.

'Always got a grudge about somethin',' he opined. 'But watch him, Vern — I'd take his advice and get me a gun.

Yuma's bound to have a spare.'

Clinton nodded and lit his smoke, admitted to himself that it would feel good to have a gun again — not because of any threat from Barnes, but — well, because he'd become so used to carrying one. It had gotten him out of a lot of scrapes — into a lot, too, he had to admit.

He looked down, surprised to find he was opening and closing his right hand, wiggling the fingers. He smiled thinly.

Fact was, he didn't feel — complete — without a six-gun on his hip . . .

★   ★   ★

Blue must have spoken to Yuma because not long after the rancher rode in from tallying his cattle on the south slope, he appeared under the ramada, and dropped a Colt in a worn holster with a bullet belt around it on to the table.

'Want no more trouble between you and Pres, but you'll need a gun . . . it's pretty old, one of the first Peacemakers, and it'll stand some doctorin'.' Yuma paused. 'I kinda get the impression you ain't exactly a stranger to the workin' of guns.'

'Know a bit about 'em,' Clinton admitted, sliding the Colt from leather. There were some worn spots where the blueing had been thinned over the years. The hammer was stiff but cocked smoothly enough, no jerks or clunks that would indicate broken lugs or a weak spring. He spun the cylinder and it moved reluctantly.

'Grips're too thick and it needs some oil and a bit of filing here and there,' he opined. 'Leather'll come good with some neatsfoot oil — but some of those cartridges look past their prime.' He indicated at least four with green verdigris showing on the brass cases, some with white scum on the lead. 'Wouldn't trust 'em to fire every time . . . Have to be leery of the new stuff, too. This old metal might not take the new powder without cracking. But I

47

can adjust loads.'

Yuma seemed hesitant, added awkwardly, 'I — I'm not lookin' for a range war, Vern.'

Clinton arched his eyebrows. 'Then I'd say you're going about things the wrong way.'

'I did it legal, that's all . . . Bracken's so arrogant he figures he can grab any land he wants.'

'He said it was open range here.'

'It was. So he had a right to build on it. But I also had a right to it and I knew he was buildin' this line camp just to keep me off — he don't *need* this range. He might have plans for it some day, but you don't play that kinda waitin' game when folk are settlin' into a valley like this.'

'So you got under his neck — and he's riled.' Yuma nodded but Clinton shook his head slowly. 'I'd be riled, too, the way you did it.'

'I filed legal!' Yuma seemed to figure that was all he needed by way of defence. 'He just left it too late.'

'Sure — but I gather you moved in and kicked his crew off, took over this fine cabin.'

'Had a right! The land was mine — and whatever was on it. Says so on the Land Deeds.'

'Letter of the law ain't always *exactly* the right thing, Yuma. You must've known how Bracken would react.'

Yuma's face was stiff, almost challenging. 'I'm still in the right.'

Clinton sighed. 'Just trying to tell you, sometimes that ain't enough — or even *right*.'

'Damnit! Whose side you on, Clinton?'

'Yours — just trying to get you to admit whatever trouble is coming, is of your own making.'

'Well, I dunno as I can use a man who thinks that way! I — I'm obliged for you steppin' in with Bracken but if you figure he's right an' I'm wrong . . .'

'I figure you're both wrong. But that's just how it is.'

After some tightlipped, heavy breathing, Yuma said, 'Then you'll be leavin'?'

Clinton's face was sober, gaze steady. 'I owe you.'

Yuma sat down across the table from Clinton. 'Not — necessarily. I'd've helped any ranny in the same situation.'

'I believe that — but you helped *me*. Which makes me obligated.'

'Look, Vern — I'll be honest. I don't want to lose you. But — if you need to salve your conscience, what you did when Bracken was here squares things far as I'm concerned — I ain't gonna try to keep you if you want to move on.'

'I'll move on when I'm ready. Now leave it at that, Yuma.'

The rancher nodded but frowned. 'You'll stay then?'

'I already said I owe you. Way I see it, you prodded Bracken when you didn't need to. That's more a mistake than 'doing wrong' but I savvy why, it got you a ready-made ranch house and corrals, even a half-finished barn — fair enough. And I don't know what happened between you and Bracken before — I'd guess that you'd gone

50

head-to-head over something and Bracken tried to squeeze you out by jumping in on this bench before you . . . Only he's a man who don't worry about what's legal and what's not, long as he gets what he wants.'

'You got that right. He wants *all* of this valley.'

'Met his kind before over the years — even when I was a kid. My pa tried to settle free range a couple times — he wasn't really the type but he wanted land of his own for the family, so he stuck his neck out. There was always someone bigger and tougher and richer who wanted just the land he was trying to settle — '

'Sounds like Bracken's kin were around even then. He's got more'n half his land by rough-stuff and buyin' off any opposition — ruined a lot of folk . . . Reckon it was my lucky day — or night — when you showed up, Vern.' He offered his right hand. 'Mighty glad to have you workin' for Flyin' Y.' When Clinton arched his eyebrows, Yuma

51

looked kind of embarrassed, added, 'I know it's a mite high-falutin', but that's my brand — always wanted a place of my own, called 'Flyin' Y'.'

'Good name,' Clinton allowed, gripping firmly with the work-calloused hand. 'You're going to have to fight for it, though.'

'I'm willin'! 'Specially if I've good back-up.'

'Good enough, lemme see what I can do with this Colt and we'll be ready to go.'

'Sure. Take your time.' Yuma started to rise, but dropped back on to the form. 'You, you got one helluva scar under your left shoulder-blade. Noticed it when I had you a'bed. Looks fairly old, but must've been a mighty bad wound.'

'Sharps Big Fifty. Luckily at extreme range or it'd blown my arm off. Still took out most of a rib and had me knocking on the Devil's door for a few weeks.'

'Back-shootin's somethin' I can't abide.' Clinton smiled crookedly, knowing the unstated question in those words. 'Yeah, it was posse lead. They had an old buffalo runner for their scout. Four years ago now.'

Yuma nodded, stood this time and walked away.

He knew he had had all the explanation he was going to get.

For now, it was all he needed.

4

Not Wanted

Tom Pardoe — 'Trapper' Tom — sheriff of the town of Wildspot — the 'wild' part referring to the nature of the countryside in the near vicinity rather than the state of the town — looked up from the stack of Wanted dodgers and shook his head.

'No one here by the name of Vern Clinton, Luke.'

Across the paper-strewn desk from the lawman, big Luke Bracken scowled and leaned forward in his chair.

'The name ain't important, Tom! He could call himself 'Abe Lincoln' for the matter of that — it's the *description* I gave you.'

Tom Pardoe, nudging sixty and with nigh on forty of those years wearing a lawman's badge, scratched at some hair in one ear that was itching. He sniffed, squinted at a well-used note book, holding it at arm's length.

'Ain't much, Luke — six-feet, plus or minus an inch or two; wide shoulders, but tends to lean slightly left — which could come from an old wound or just from drawing his gun fast lots of times — that lean might make a difference to the speed, I guess. Slick Saunders used the trick, they say.' *And so had 'Trapper' Tom Pardoe in his early town-taming days . . . only he wasn't saying.*

'Well, that oughta tell you somethin'! It's a gun-fighter's stance — Backs up my contention he's on the dodge.'

Pardoe flicked his tired grey eyes at the rancher and went on reading from his notes. 'Lean as a rail — burned dark like old leather, which means livin' plenty outdoors . . . and that covers a few thousand cowpokes between here and San Francisco, Luke.'

Bracken thumped one large fist on the edge of the desk. There was a creak of wood and Pardoe frowned. 'You bust my desk, the County'll bill you for a new one, Luke.'

'The hell with your desk! Look, I'm tellin' you — Yuma's hired himself a gunfighter. If he ain't among your Wanted dodgers, only means he's been smart enough to stay clear of the law. Or you ain't keepin' 'em up-to-date.'

'Or he's been mighty lucky.'

'Yeah — all right! But I swear he's a killer, Tom. I know a killer's eyes when I see 'em, an' he was just itchin' to let me have it with that Greener.'

Pardoe sighed and closed his note-book. 'He could have a lot of company there. Can't find him here, Luke, and if he ain't broke any law, then Yuma's entitled to hire him . . . Might just be a tough cowboy, plenty of them around.'

'By hell, I tell you I won't be votin' for you next election, Tom! You can be damn sure of that!'

'Sorry to hear that, Luke. But won't much matter, 'cause I'm takin' retirement and you'll have to vote in someone new.'

'You won't be any loss to this County,' growled the big rancher standing fast so that the backs of his legs knocked over his straightback chair. He made no effort to pick it up, hitched at his gunbelt and turned towards the door.

'I'll damn well put my own man in — see how this lousy town likes *that*!'

'Luke — you quit roustin' Yuma over this. I've had a request from Sheriff Adams in Walpole to check out any new drifters, so I'll mebbe ride out sometime and look-over this Clinton feller. So far, he seems OK — don't you start any trouble.'

Hand on the door latch, Bracken glared at the sheriff. 'Yuma's already started it!'

'Now, you ease up, Luke, or . . . '

The door slammed behind the angry rancher and Pardoe heaved a sigh, reached for his old charred pipe and the battered humidor of tobacco, shaking his head slowly.

'Greed — one of the Seven Deadly

Sins — and you got all of 'em, Luke, every — last — one!'

* * *

The Cross Iron was the biggest spread in this part of the country and Luke Bracken aimed to keep it that way — and grow even bigger.

He was still in a bad mood after his interview with Old Tom Pardoe earlier. He ought to have known that old badge-toter wouldn't get off his ass and make a proper search for this Clinton — or whatever the hell his name was. All he had to do was send a few telegraphs, ask around the country, describe Clinton! Bracken was *sure* the man was a gunfighter. *And if Yuma figured he could get away with that* . . . Anyway, he had set a man on the ridge overlooking Big Cat Bench — what used to be *his* bench, dammit! — a man up there with a good pair of field glasses, just to see how this Vern Clinton behaved . . .

He ought to be returning pretty soon now: it was getting on towards sundown. Even as he thought this, he parted the curtains of the front window and saw a rider skidding to a halt down by the corrals. He recognized Morgan Bragg through the dust and saw the man hurrying toward the house, swinging the field glasses by their shoulder strap.

Bracken wrenched open the front door and was waiting at the top of the porch steps when Bragg arrived.

'Goddammit, Morg! Those are German glasses! Cost me a small fortune to bring 'em into the country! Be more careful with 'em. They should be in their case, anyway.'

'Sorry, boss. Left the ridge in kind of a hurry. Case is still up there, but it'll be OK! I'll get it in the mornin'.'

Luke scowled. 'You might not have such an easy chore, come mornin'! Did you see that drifter? Yuma put him to work . . . ?'

Morg Bragg was a solid man through

the shoulders, only medium tall, and from Bracken's position at the top of the stairs, he looked quite squat. He had a round face, fringed by dusty stubble, hard eyes with lots of creases at the corners from long years of outdoor work — and scarred knuckles on his thick-fingered hands — from different work, like hammering men to do his will — or Bracken's, mostly.

Now he lifted a boot on to the bottom step and leaned on his bent knee, smiling thinly.

'Yuma ain't put him to work — leastways, not what you or me'd call work.'

'Never mind the commentary, just tell me what he was doing.'

Bragg's smile widened. 'How you like to hear he set up a long line of targets on a deadfall — stones, twigs, couple old mugs, some balls of screwed-up paper — nothin' too big, then he shot the hell out of 'em in the blink of an eye! Not just once — but over and over — Yuma and the other two just stood there, mouths hangin', catchin' flies.'

The man's a gunfighter, no getting away from that! Yuma, packing a pipe carefully, tamping down the tobacco just right, scraped a vesta into flame and puffed rhythmically and slowly, making sure the pipe would draw well. He needed its calming properties as he once again thought about his new hand, Vern Clinton. *Thought again? Hell, he hadn't been able to stop thinking about the way Clinton had shot those hastily-arranged targets all to hell!*

It was something to see, exciting even — but, Yuma being essentially a law-abiding man, he wondered just who the hell was this man who had walked across a desert and climbed mountains to get here.

'Pres is right,' he murmured half-aloud. 'He has to be on the run. No reg'lar man would even attempt what he done, 'less he was forced to it.'

He felt a small tremor in his hands: the man was hell on wheels! Look how he beat-up Pres, when he must've been near exhausted after his desert crossing and the rough treatment he had received. Then — then — squaring-up to Luke Bracken — and *now* . . .

Despite the cool of the evening, there was sweat on Yuma's brow. Abruptly, he turned back to the ramada where Clinton sat smoking at the end of the supper table as he oiled the old Colt he had tuned and shot so devastatingly.

Still, as Pres had commented, somewhat sourly, '*Targets can't shoot back!*'

But Yuma had seen several gunfighters over the years, had worked alongside one a long time ago in El Paso, and he knew a good deal about men who lived by the gun. Vern Clinton was just such a man — but Yuma was a mite leery about asking too much . . . He strolled across, puffing on his pipe, he held it down at his side and nodded to Clinton who, as usual, seemed calm and relaxed as he rubbed an oily rag over the Colt.

'Some shootin' earlier.'

'Kinda out of practice.'

Yuma looked at him sharply but saw the man wasn't joshing: he was making a flat statement.

'Well — you must be half-brother to a bolt of lightnin' when you're *in* practice.'

Clinton lifted his head, smiled faintly. 'There're plenty like that, Yuma.'

'Not around here.'

Clinton's eyes studied the rancher's homely face and watched him puff at his pipe — but the tobacco had gone cold, apparently. Yuma glared at the pipe, pushed it into his shirt pocket.

'I didn't realize I was hirin' a top gunfighter.'

'You think that's what I am?'

'If you ain't — you have been.'

Clinton remained silent while he slid the cylinder back into the frame and locked it. Satisfied with the way it spun, he began pushing cartridges into the chambers.

'You've a right to know — I already told you that old shoulder scar was from a posse's bullet. Well, a different posse was on my tail and drove me across the desert — and here I am.' When Yuma said nothing, Vern added, 'Or am I . . . ?'

'I could sure use a man like you, Vern — but — well, I'm mostly law-abidin'. I wouldn't want to turn round one mornin' and find my land claim cancelled and I'm in court, bein' charged with harbourin' a — outlaw.'

'Sure not, but I'm a long — long — way from where I had my trouble, Yuma. I'm pretty sure they think I'm dead — not that that'd stop Sheriff Adams from hunting around . . . '

'*Adams?*' cut in Yuma. 'From the Panhandle some wheres, ain't he . . . ? Yeah, thought so — heard of him and, like you say, he has a long memory.'

'And then some.'

'He got his knife into you?'

'Into any man who escapes his custody — and not many do.'

'But you did . . . '

There was a question there and Clinton had to decide — now — whether he answered it or not . . .

'Blue's got supper about ready, mebbe we could talk after we eat?'

Yuma knew Clinton needed time to think and was willing enough to wait, give him a chance to consider things. He knew instinctively that this gun-fighter wouldn't be making up a bunch of lies: he'd just be deciding how much he should tell of his story — in case there was a possibility of involving Yuma further if anything should go wrong . . .

And no man on the run could guarantee it wouldn't.

* * *

After a quiet supper all four gathered around for their usual after-meal smoke and evening talk. Yuma wasn't sure Clinton wanted that big an audience, so had said quietly, before supper,

'I'll have some small chores for Pres and Blue to do.'

'It's OK. If I'm staying on, be best if

they know who they're working with.'

'Up to you . . . But Pres is loose-tongued when he gets a coupla whiskies under his belt. Kinda nasty, too.'

Clinton frowned and nodded gently. 'OK — Blue can stay or not.'

After Pres went off with bad grace to snug-down the newest broke-in horse for the night, Clinton said quietly,

'For a start, name's not Vern Clinton, but that don't matter. You don't need to know my real one.'

'Guess not.' But Yuma sounded a mite disappointed.

Blue shrugged, looking impatient to hear this drifter's story.

'OK, won't say I was born with a fast draw, but after my pa died and I — tangled with the men who killed him — well, they had friends and I had to make a run for it. I stole a horse, which was just what they wanted. Down on the Panhandle, you hang hoss-thieves when you catch up with 'em — or did at that time . . . I gave 'em the slip, fell in

66

with a bunch of rough fellers who made their money outta selling cattle — other peoples' cattle.'

'A hoss thief *and* a rustler!' thought Yuma with a mild shock.

Clinton continued, the words coming more easily now, once he'd started.

'It was easy money — anything I'd earned before that had made me sweat a bucket of blood for every lousy nickel — and they were few and far between. Riding with that bunch was just the life to be attractive to a fifteen-sixteen year old . . .'

Yuma and Blue exchanged looks when they heard that — they hadn't suspected Clinton might be a career outlaw. But there it was: he'd just admitted it and they looked at him now with even more attention and eagerness to hear his story.

There was quite a long silence while he thought about things, and the others grew restless.

Then he snapped out of his reverie and said quickly, 'There was a feller with a reputation for being a fast gun in that gang: 'Tip' someone but most folk called him 'Rapido' . . . '

'Hell!' exclaimed Blue. 'I seen him once! In Wichita! 'Rapido' was a damn good nickname — he was the fastest man ever to ride them old cattle trails.'

Clinton nodded soberly. 'That's him — he took a shine to me, made me practise till I thought my arm'd break — then he'd massage it with neatsfoot oil and turpentine, wrap it in hot cloths — and in the morning, make me start practising all over again . . . Yeah — Rapido . . . taught me all he knew. Seems a helluva long time ago now.' His voice drifted off into introspection, but only briefly. His face went kind of tight as he continued: 'He was truly the fastest gun alive till he met someone faster . . . '

'Faster!' exclaimed Yuma, shaking his head in disbelief. 'That possible . . . ?'

Blue was more to the point. 'Who?'

Clinton's sober gaze pinned him.

'Me.'

5

Wild Days

There had been a close shave with a herd of steers coming up from Tucson. The trail boss had kept a bunch of armed men riding parallel with the herd, or behind, but out of sight. They followed the dust, were saddle-ready at all times, guns loaded for bear — or would-be rustlers.

Rapido knew nothing of the ghost guardians, saw only that close-packed herd and only seven riders sweating it along.

Wade figured it looked too easy, and Buzzy Gann tugged at his beard with rapid movements, a sure sign he was agitated. Tarco, the breed, dozed, awaiting a decision: he had no opinions.

'Four of us and seven of them, Rap,' Wade pointed out.

'You gettin' scarder the older you are?' growled Rapido and Wade shut up — lately Rapido had been on a short fuse and had actually gunwhipped one of the gang so badly he needed to stay in hospital. Which was why there were only four of them now, eyeing off the lumbering herd.

They had run into 'bad luck' — that's what Rapido called it, but it was an ambush — when they hit a Wells Fargo Express Depot that supposedly was holding a big payroll. Two men had been killed and Rapido had been shot in the head. It was a deep bullet crease and they got him to a doctor, slipping into a small trail town after dark by back streets.

The sawbones wanted Rapido to stay in his infirmary for a few days but the fastest gun alive would have none of that. He thrust a fistful of money into the medic's hand and said,

'My time will be better spent elsewhere, Doc.' He winked heavily and the old man knew he was talking about

70

another 'job' but shook his head slowly.

'Sir, the bone has been depressed. It must be pressing on part of your brain — Activity, particularly hard riding and, yes, even over-indulgence in alcohol may give you violent headaches — and — worse. Wild mood changes . . . '

'I don't want to know about the 'worse', doc,' Rapido told him obstinately. 'Headaches I can deal with — *Muchas gracias*, and *adios*.' He jerked his bandaged head at the door. 'Let's go, you *hombres*, I feel like a drink . . . '

'Good God, man, haven't you heard a word I said!' exclaimed the doctor.

'Every single one, Doc — and din' like 'em.' He laughed, sounding almost drunk right now. 'Sorry!'

He led the way out and the medical man grabbed Wade's arm, him being last in line.

'You look intelligent, young man — I implore you, make that fool take it easy! I know who he is, but he may not realize that that head wound is quite serious . . . I don't want to alarm you, but — in one of his bouts of pain, he could be irrational — and violent — extremely violent. It may not be possible to control him.'

'See what I can do, Doc,' said Wade worriedly, hurrying after the others.

There was nothing he could do. Nothing any of them could do. Rapido had bouts of violent headaches and to treat them he drank heavily, trying to numb them with the raw frontier booze. In Wade's opinion, the booze only made things worse and they quickly learned to stay out of Rapido's way until he passed out — *then* it was anybody's guess what shape he would be in when he came round . . .

But he seemed to slowly improve. It was almost a month after receiving the headwound — healed nicely now, with a puckered pink scar across his scalp — when Rapido woke them all in the middle of the night, camped out in the Superstition Mountains, and announced their next job.

'Boys, I'm gonna make us all rich! *Rich* rich, I mean — We're gonna make our fortune by robbin' the bank at Huachuca!'

His words drove the last dregs of sleep from them.

'Huachuca?' echoed Buzzy Gann. 'Judas, did I hear right? That's the most protected bank in Arizona, everyone knows that! It services the silver mines and there's at least a dozen guards, all with scatterguns, and the fastest broncs in the Territory! They reckon they can run sun-up to sundown, then go chasin' a bunch of mares!'

Rapido grinned tightly. 'All hogwash! Just *talk*! No bank could keep that level of protection all the time.'

'I've seen that bank and it's crawling with guards Rap', said Wade quietly.

'Yeah? They tell you they were guards? They struttin' around with guns over their shoulders like the sentries at the Fort? Give you a salute? Huh?'

'No, but they're easy to pick, loungin' around in shadowy corners, trying to look like waiting customers.'

'Well, you sure ain't ever gonna be rich,' cut in Rapido sourly, glaring hard at the young gunfighter.

And that bleak look made Gann even more worried — everyone knew how Rapido favoured the kid — or had done . . .

When asked, Tarco shrugged, pointed at Rapido. 'He the boss.'

'That makes two for, two against — what do we do to swing the vote one way or another?'

'How about we forget the whole damn thing?' Buzzy suggested and for a wild moment, Wade thought Rapido was going to draw on Gann — Gann did, too, and paled noticeably. 'Aw, wait-up, Rap! I mean — four of us agin all them trained guards just bustin' to show off how good they are . . . ?'

Rapido smiled, dropped an arm around Gann's shoulders.

'I'll show you how to do it — and them guards, whatever they're like, won't do a damn thing. You game to try?'

There was no arguing with the man —

But he surprised them all. They walked into the Huachuca bank like any cowhands in from one of the outlying ranches or a trail herd bedding-down out on the flats.

Wade's sharp gaze flicked here and there, picked out the guards trying to make themselves look like part of the furniture. Confidently, Rapido led the way across the foyer to where a well-dressed lady with high-piled coiffered hair and a somewhat wary welcoming smile asked if she could help them.

'Why, sure, li'l lady,' Rapido told her in his best West Texas accent, smiling. 'Me an' my pards'd like to see the President.' He lowered his voice. 'A small matter of depositin' some gold coins — ' He shook the canvas bag of old rusted iron washers they had collected from an abandoned silver mine. He winked at the woman who was definitely interested now. 'Lot more where they come from and we'd like to have your boss draw up an agreement, between the four of us

75

and the bank for future deposits from our mine . . . '

She was smiling widely now, lifted the flap to allow them to file in. They were in the Banker's office within minutes — and he and his receptionist were under their guns. Both were on the verge of fainting, but Rapido gave his orders calmly, telling the man what he wanted from the safe.

'Now you just call your man in an' tell him to go get it and bring it back here . . . ' Rapido stepped close to the trembling woman and placed his gun barrel under her left ear. She gasped and he smiled as he held her upright with his other hand. 'Relax, gal. Your boss does what he's told, you got nothin' to worry about. Ah, yeah, almost forgot: tell your guards to come on in, one at a time, but leave their scatter-guns . . . '

Wade and Buzzy and Tarco had to admit, Rapido's crazy plan worked like a charm — but the seven guards were all going to wake up with hefty headaches from the gun butts that struck each one behind the right ear as they entered.

Riding high on excitement, Rapido commandeered a stage coach, just loading at the depot across the street. They took two fat businessmen with them and the wife of one, and the bug-eyed driver, Jinglebob Swain, who whipped the team and roared out of town.

The stageline agent had a message to give the groggy guards and the bleary-eyed sheriff when he finally came to.

'Don't follow — unless you bring shovels for diggin' graves.'

Reluctantly, when it was known who the hostages were, the message was taken seriously and everyone waited in town for some news. It was hours later when the stumbling exhausted passengers appeared, making their way to town, dusty, thirsty — and bare-foot.

'No use tryin' to follow,' one of the men gasped after some water and resting his blistered feet in a bowl of Condies crystal solution. 'They'll be outta the Territory by now . . . '

Well — not quite.

In the boot, amongst the luggage the passengers had left, the robbers found four bottles of imported Scotch whisky — one bottle each. Wade was not much of a drinker, especially when 'working', and took only a couple of snorts and then Rapido snatched the bottle from him.

'Can't let it go to waste.'

'Better go easy, Rap. Remember what that sawbones said.'

'What sawbones?' Rap laughed harshly, drank deeply and then went to where Jinglebob Swain was sitting, looking despondent at all that good liquor flowing — but none of it down his gullet.

He looked hopefully at the others, licking his lips.

Rapido, swaying, bleary-eyed, held out a half-bottle. 'For bein' such a good sport, Jingo. Take it with you up to the drivin' seat an' let's get underway!'

That they did, and Jinglebob, who had never tasted the smoothness or latent potency of single-malt whisky before, emptied his share quickly.

The stage clattered along the twisting, undulating trail and Swain began to sing, then changed it into a series of warwhoops, finally standing on his seat and whipping up the already straining team. His judgement was way off and he drove clear off the ridge trail and overturned the stage on a steep embankment.

Luckily the harness snapped and the team broke free and headed for the brush. Tarco, part-Mex, part-Iroquois Indian, climbed up through the shattered door somehow and, kneeling, rode the sliding, jerking vehicle all the way down the grassy, rock-studded slope — cutting loose with a wild warwhoop his warrior father had taught him long ago. Then it shied off a large boulder and sent him flying through the air to crash into the boulder's twin.

The others struggled out of the

wrecked coach, checking themselves for hurts, but there was nothing serious, though Rapido's scalp wound had broken open and blood streamed down one side of his face. It didn't seem to bother him except he squinted a lot: maybe from the liquor.

They stood around the rock where Tarco lay, twisted like a pretzel. Buzzy, the last to climb out of the wreckage, held up a half-full bottle. 'We're OK! Enough medicine to get us goin' again,' he slurred, laughing with his crooked mouth all out of shape and bloody.

He swigged, stumbled over and handed the bottle to Rapido who drank and passed it to Wade. But Wade had had enough of both the whisky and the drunken shenanigans. The bottle neck was all bloody from Buzzy's mouth, too. So, he casually pushed the bottle aside as Rapido offered it. It fell and smashed against the slowly-turning iron tyre of one of the coach's rear wheels.

Buzzy and Rapido stared down at the broken glass and the whisky soaking into the ground. Rapido looked up slowly, face ugly now, with drink and boiling over in genuine anger.

'You stupid damn kid! Still twenny miles to Bisbee an' now we gotta do it without a drink! An' my head's fit to bust!'

He rubbed vigorously at his forehead, wincing, smearing the blood across his grimacing face. Wade refrained from making any smart remark he may have thought of.

'Let's steady-up and look for the money. Must be somewhere in the wreckage . . .' He turned towards the wreck but was spun about by the shoulder, staggering. Rapido's big meaty hand caught him across the side of the head and knocked him sprawling. He grunted, blinking, pulled himself erect, blood trickling from his mouth and nostrils. Rapido stood with boots spread, hands slightly out from his sides. Buzzy paled, grabbed at the swaying gunfighter.

'Jesus, Rap! Easy man! No need for this — Let's see that head wound and we'll sort things out . . . '

Rapido's Colt rammed into Buzzy's midriff and blasted twice, the shots muffled. Buzzy jerked back, fell, clutching at his bloody wounds. His agony-filled eyes stared accusingly at the gunman as he toppled on to his face. Wade dropped to one knee beside Buzzy, snapped his head up.

'Judas priest, Rap! You never give him a chance!'

Rapido was sniffing, eyes wilder than Wade had ever seen them. He grimaced and returned the smoking gun to his holster and resumed his gun-fighting stance.

'I'm givin' *you* a chance!'

'Chris'sake, Rap! What the hell're you thinkin'? That damn booze addled your brain? Settle down and we'll — '

'Draw!'

All through the long months of lessons, Rapido had instilled into Wade that he *never, ever,* called a man out twice. He had slapped Wade silly a dozen times when the kid didn't react instantly to the sudden and unexpected '*Draw!*' that could come at any time. *Any time* . . . . But he had learned the lesson well.

Now, when Rapido roared the word Wade's gun was instantly in his hand, blazing — only this time, it wasn't practice blanks he was shooting, they were real .45 calibre lead bullets. Two of them cut Rapido down where he stood, his gun not quite clear of leather.

The kid knelt beside him in a flash, gun holstered, face contorted, still dripping blood from his nostrils. It mingled with that spurting from the holes in Rapido's chest.

'Aw, hell, Rap! I — I just . . .'

Rapido was fading quickly but he lifted his gun hand and tried to grasp Wade's. The kid gripped with him but felt the life draining from Rapido — fast. 'Good — pupil — kid — g-good — ' the dying gunfighter rasped and his head fell loosely to the side . . .

★   ★   ★

Yuma, watching the face of the man he knew as Vern Clinton, said, 'Helluva thing, Vern.'

'Bothered me for a long time.'

'Hell, you din' have to spread the word you beat Rapido!' said Blue. 'Not that way . . . ' He stopped and eased back when the cold eyes settled on his face: his outrage was dying fast . . . but Clinton remained calm.

'No — that damn Jinglebob, the stage driver, did it for me. He saw the whole thing — he spread the word. I quit Arizona but somethin' like that can follow you around for years — and it did, growin' a bit each time it was told, distorted, till I hardly recognized it: made me out to be the original mad-dog killer.'

'What happened . . . ?' Blue asked more quietly, and Yuma leaned forward, too, eager to hear the rest . . .

★   ★   ★

Wade caught one of the stage team and rode away from the wreck, once he knew the driver was all right. *He looked for the money but it must've been trapped underneath the heavy coach — anyway, sickened by what had happened, he decided he wanted no more of this outlawry . . .*

The driver no doubt drank himself stupid every night for years after on the telling of what he had seen that day *. . . when Rapido, fastest gun alive, had gone down to his protégé's gun . . .*

Wade suffered because of it. Everywhere he went folk stared, pointed him out and, inevitably, some self-assured, strutting town bully called him out. Folk ran from everywhere to see the gunfights — but most missed out, weren't even in position before it was all over, the kid walking away from the newly-dead man lying in the mud or dust.

He rode on to other towns, left five more dead men behind him: he knew by then a lot more were ahead of him . . .

The gunfights became monotonous.

He tried all kinds of disguises but usually someone turned up in the town where he was and recognized him.

And the guns barked and he rode out, weary of the killing, but damned if he was going to back down from any challenge. *Rapido had taught him that, too.*

Over the years he did manage to go for a long time occasionally without anyone challenging him. He took regular range-country jobs on ranches, freight lines, riding shotgun, once or twice for a stageline, even took a law badge in some boom town that needed taming and local law couldn't handle it alone.

He never missed a day, though, practising his draw. He knew it was the only way to stay alive. He enjoyed a drink but was careful to stay sober at all times, and was happy with obliging women. He never dropped his guard completely. *Just in case someone recognized him . . .*

It happened sometimes in the most

unexpected places. Once he had escorted a high-class *señorita* to church when he was working south of the Border on her father's *rancho*.

When the Mass was over and they were leaving, there was a man with silver conchas flashing on his vest and black leather chaps, standing four-square solid beside the handsome buggy that had brought Wade and the girl to the church.

'You do not wear your gun to church, I see, *señor*,' the man said smiling. 'That is correct, of course, but I 'ave persuaded the *muchacho* you left to watch your *transportadora*' — he indicated the buggy — 'to allow me to look into it.' He reached behind without turning and brought out Wade's gun rig, tossing it so it landed in the dust at his feet.

'Now — you 'ave your *pistola* and I 'ave mine. It is time, eh? A shame to disturb the peace on a Sunday but — ' He shrugged elaborately. 'I give you a count of five to buckle on your gun,

Señor Wade . . . '

The girl looked at him sharply. 'Wade? That is not your name . . . '

'I'll explain later, Dolores. Move to the side, *querida* — pronto.'

He stooped and scooped up the gun rig, started to buckle it about him when the challenger shouted '*Cinco!*' — making it a very fast count — and went for his ornate guns.

Wade snatched his Colt from the holster, letting the bullet belt's weight drag the leather away from the gun as he lifted, and blasted the Mexican, even as the man fired.

Wade lurched into the girl behind him and heard her gasp. He spun, ignoring for the moment the burning pain across his ribs as she fell. The bullet meant for him had barely touched him but had gone past to kill Dolores . . .

It had been a long, long hard ride outdistancing the group of *pistoleros* Dolores' father sent after him.

It was a year before he could show

his face in Texas, even, and then he rode well away from the Border, up to the Panhandle where there were big herds gathering and plenty of work on far-flung ranches with lonesome ranges where he could lose himself — *and do his daily practice* . . .

On a trail drive bound for Abilene, Kansas, they over-nighted at a north Texas town called Ballard, named after the rich rancher who had settled the area and now owned almost the entire County. He had a wild son, Gavin, not yet twenty, arrogant, flashy, and who couldn't hold his liquor without looking for a fight.

Old Man Ballard hired a man of some gun prowess to stand guard over Gavin at such times. The man was named Ross and when the kid took a dislike to Wade in the saloon and prodded and prodded until the guns were drawn, Ross stepped in quickly and tried to backshoot Wade as Gavin lay dying on the floor. Wade took Ross's bullet across the left hip, shot the man through the head. Smoke curling around him, he glared at the staring faces in the suddenly silent saloon.

'You all saw who started it.'

There were murmurings but no one said anything intelligible. The sheriff sure did, though, when he arrived and saw who the main victim was; he rose from examining Gavin's corpse and swung up the sawn-off shotgun he had brought, covering Wade.

'Lift your hands, gunfighter!'

'The kid wouldn't let it go, Sheriff,' Wade protested. 'He pushed it to the draw. Ask anyone here.'

No one spoke up and the sheriff, smiling crookedly, jerked his head towards the batwings. 'You march on down to my cellblock, mister. We'll see what Mr Ballard has to say about this.'

* * *

The trial was a sham. Old Man Ballard didn't take kindly to some dirty dung-smelling trailhand killing his son.

He was told by some that Gavin had definitely started it — the town had had little time for the cocky young Ballard — but they didn't press things with the rancher. They had to live here and knew from past experience he only listened to things he wanted to hear.

'Gavin started it?' Ballard snapped when the sheriff hesitantly mentioned witnesses. 'I can find at least seven men who witnessed the confrontation, who say this killer prodded Gavin until he was riled enough to go for his gun. But Gavin just wasn't good enough, I guess. That might count a lot with the scum who killed him, but he'll find out it won't keep him from a rope necktie . . . '

The necktie party came close to succeeding — a half-drunken mob, again whipped up by Ballard dollars — but the sheriff had been leery enough to hastily form a group of temporary deputies, mostly from Wade's trail herd — and nipped the lynching in the bud.

'Best if we go to trial, Mr Ballard,' he told the irate rancher nervously.

'Look for another job, Sheriff. You're finished here.'

Wade was sentenced to ten years on the rockpile in the County penitentiary.

'Got us a special train to take you hard-heads up there,' the judge told him with the others headed for the same destination. 'We call it the 'Rockpile Express'.'

The train ride was just as hellish as Wade had imagined. And that was just the start.

It seemed that the Warden was named 'Ballard', too — the late Gavin's uncle to be exact . . .

Somehow, Wade endured — survived, might be a better word — three desperate years before they decided to close down this particular penitentiary and send the inmates to another, already overcrowded prison at a place aptly named Hell's Gate.

Ballard was financing railroads now as well as monopolizing the cattle business, and was happy to lay the new spur track to Hell's Gate.

But Mr Ballard lost a good deal of money on that run: the tracks had been laid using convict labour and many of the tie-spikes had been shortened by as much as half their length, so that after a dozen carriages and flatbed freight wagons had passed over a certain section, the rails bounced violently and the ties popped loose with devastating results.

The loosened rails jumped off the ties and then it was too late for the startled engineer to do anything as the locomotive began to tilt. He yelled but it was lost in the screech and clatter of crumpling metal and roaring jets of steam as the Rockpile Express rolled down the bank, the couplings holding long enough to drag the rolling stock behind, then snapping like a volley from a firing squad.

All just out of sight of the prison.

* * *

'You must lead a charmed life,' Yuma opined as Clinton took a long pause in his story.

The man smiled crookedly. 'I was lucky — took a few hefty knocks but came round first, found the others mostly dead. I changed clothes with a guard who was pretty much mangled — figured they might think it was me — and got out of there before the rescue team arrived. When eventually I came to the desert I figured that was the end of the trail for me.'

'But you made it across — and here you are.'

Yuma produced a bottle of rye and poured drinks all round. There were no toasts, just Yuma and Blue watching Clinton. After the second drink, Yuma cleared his throat.

'I'd sure like you workin' for me, Vern — But I gotta be honest. I guess you're used to fightin' wages, and I won't be able to run to that.'

Clinton didn't even look at him, rolled a cigarette, then lifted his gaze to Yuma's worried face as he struck a match across the table.

'I reckon I been treated pretty good

so far here. Like your cooking, Blue. If you can guarantee me plenty of grub at the standard you've set so far, and you, Yuma, if you can pay me the usual forty-and-found, I reckon I know enough about ranching to earn it.'

Yuma was surprised but quickly splashed rye into the glasses again. Blue nodded, smiling.

'I'll cook up a storm — startin' with breakfast.' And they drank a brief toast to welcome Clinton as a member of the Flying Y crew.

'Dollar buys your gun, huh?'

Yuma looked up as Pres suddenly appeared around the corner of the cabin: Clinton wondered how long the man had been there, how much he had heard . . .

Pres looked at all three. 'Don't bother pourin' me any — I won't drink to *him*!'

He wheeled away into the darkness and they heard him stomping angrily.

'Think you might've just lost a friend,' Blue said sardonically.

Clinton looked off into the darkness. 'I've known a few men like that.' Clinton said. 'Chip-on-the-shoulder, pigheaded. But they're all dead now.'

6

Bounty Hunter

Pres Barnes told Yuma right after breakfast he had to go see the dentist in town and the rancher stared levelly. Pres tilted his jaw stubbornly, then lifted a hand and rubbed gently at one side — carefully pushing his tongue across so the cheek bulged.

'Been givin' me a heap of trouble. Gettin' smacked around by that drifter din' help any.'

'You asked for the smackin' around,' Yuma said, unsympathetically. 'Lucky he never shot you.'

Pres coloured 'Yeah, an' that's another thing — I don't much care workin' with a damn gunfighter.'

'Pres — I knew you had your ear hangin' out a mile while we were talkin'. You've been a pain in the butt for a long time.'

'It's this damn tooth, I tell you — I gotta see about it.'

'Yeah, well you go on into town, Pres — And take your warbag, too — I see only trouble, you stayin' on.'

Pres Barnes's jaw dropped. 'You — you're firin' me?'

'Let's call it payin' you off, Pres — I'll give you a note to the bank and you can pick up your money there.'

'You're ditchin' me in favour of that gunslinger!'

'I admit I'll get more use out of him, Pres, but you stay and you'll only make trouble — and I've got enough of that.'

'Well, you *an'* Blue an' sure as blazes, that gunnie, can all go to hell!'

Yuma merely nodded as Pres shouted it out and then stormed back into the cabin for his warbag.

Later, watching Pres whip and spur his mount out of the yard, Clinton said, 'That on account of me?'

'On account of Pres bein' the miserable son of a bitch he is — He's had ten jobs in this valley in just over a year. I gave him a chance but — He listened in, too, while you were talkin' to Blue an' me, but don't worry about it.'

Watching the cowboy ride over the rise, Clinton, said, quietly, 'Whatever you say.' But he didn't sound too sure.

Yuma frowned as Clinton picked up some lumber and walked back towards the barn where he was constructing a big plank door with Blue.

Yuma scrubbed a hand around his stubbled jaw.

He hoped Pres wouldn't stir up anything in town . . .

But that's exactly what Pres Barnes did — or tried to. He collected his money from the bank all right, swore about it being so measly, then went to the saloon and downed several whiskies. He asked after Amelia, one of the bar girls.

'Gone,' the 'keep told him, drying shotglasses on a grey cloth. 'And took that black eye you gave her with her.'

Pres flushed, downed his drink and stomped out. In the sunshine, watching the town's traffic and its citizens move about on Main, Pres let his gaze rest on the *Law Office* sign on its rusted chains, swinging a little in the hot breeze. Impulsively, he crossed the street and walked in without knocking.

Tom Pardoe was packing fresh tobacco into his humidor, glanced up, squinting at Pres silhouetted against the door. 'Just oiled that knocker, too,' Pardoe allowed, but it went right by Pres who said without preamble,

'That feller Yuma's got workin' for him out at Big Cat Bench — Vern Clinton — there any kinda reward out for him?'

Pardoe took in Pres's attitude, recognized the cocky young cowboy was on the prod over something, went on packing the metal jar with tobacco. 'Not as I know of. He ain't wanted for anythin' on any dodger I've got.'

Pres leaned on the front of the desk, kind of towering above Pardoe who sat back in his chair now. 'Stand straight — or siddown, Pres.'

Pres merely backed a foot away from the desk and straightened slowly. 'That's cos you looked under 'Clinton' — but mebbe that ain't his name.'

Pardoe waited, knowing Pres wanted him to ask what the man's name *was*.

Pres curled a lip when the old lawman remained silent. 'I ain't sure — but I think 'Wade' is part of it. He told Yuma an' Blue some story: he's a gunfighter, prodded some rich rancher's kid into goin' for his gun and nailed him. The Old Man got him ten years on the rockpile . . . 'Course he says the rancher framed him: the kid did all the proddin'.'

Pardoe was interested now but tried to keep his seamed old face blank. 'Uh-huh.'

'Well, he escaped — I dunno where, he never said. Panhandle someplace — but it was a train wreck south of the desert, anyway.'

'And he crossed the desert, came

here to our beautiful law-abidin' County and found hisself a ranch job. Sound like an escaped convict to you, Pres?'

'Well — yeah! Good way to hide out — anyways, why don't you look at your dodgers again — try 'Wade'.'

'Lookin' for some fast money, are you, kid? But you want me to bring him in and you'll collect for havin' spotted him, right?'

Pres looked uncomfortable, said nothing.

Sheriff Pardoe shook his head slowly. 'I was aimin' to take a look at this mystery man, anyway — Luke Bracken was in stirrin' things up about him, too. *And* I got a wire from a sheriff who'd like me to check on any new arrivals.'

Barnes looked alarmed. 'Bracken ain't claimin' the reward, too, is he? Hell, he don't need it . . .'

Pardoe lifted one of his surprisingly slim and unblemished hands. 'You sure got a one-track mind, ain't you, boy. Well, you just go hibernate for a while and I'll go check out this feller — I come back an' I might or might not tell you what I found out.'

Pres Barnes didn't like being ordered about by an old man, lawman or not — but he was cautious: folk reckoned everything said about Pardoe and his gun in his helling-around days, was gospel. Even if only half was true, he was no one to mess with.

*　*　*

Blue and Clinton were two planks short for the big barn door. They had counted and measured all right, but two of the ready-cut planks available had such warps in them that it would be a waste of good ten-penny nails fixing them to the cross bar of the door frame.

The only solution was to cut two new ones.

Bracken had obviously planned to extend this line camp into a small, self-supporting ranch in the future and had had a sawpit dug into the side of the slope. A longtooth crosscut blade was already fixed in position and it was only a matter of tossing a coin to see who went down into the pit, and who was the lucky one who got the top deck, working the saw in the open for the first shift.

Vern Clinton lost and Blue rubbed his gnarled hands together as he climbed on to the platform and tested the saw's teeth. 'Ready when you are — Lucky!'

Clinton scowled, removed his shirt and tied a neckerchief over his hair — it would keep some of the sawdust off him but he would sweat buckets and be plastered with a thick layer of wood particles in minutes, on the wrong end of that l-o-n-g saw blade.

'Change after we do the first plank, OK?' he called.

Blue made some sort of sound but it might or might not have been an affirmative. Then, still swearing, Clinton grabbed the saw handle and Blue yanked upwards right away, the steel ringing, a

104

fine spray of sawdust flying into Clinton's face, as the blade chewed the first inch into the weathered log they were to cut the planks from . . . each was to be ten feet long, a foot wide, and at least an inch thick.

They would still be here by sundown, Clinton reckoned, bitterly.

But the chore went faster than expected, the saw very sharp — never having been used before — and it fairly sliced through the log, but required a lot of effort.

So they swapped places after the first heavy plank thudded to the dirt, though Blue tried to hedge by saying he could brew a cup of coffee first — but Yuma put paid to that by bringing them down a pot already brewed and a couple of tin mugs.

They had just finished when Sheriff Pardoe rode in on his well-known Appaloosa mare.

Blue glanced sharply as Clinton stiffened, then looked around quickly. 'Where the hell's my shirt?' he rapped.

Blue gestured. 'Hanging on the low branch of yonder tree. Sun was on it when I hung it there — figured it'd sweeten it up as well as dry it off.'

He was surprised when Clinton cursed and strode quickly across and started to put on the shirt over the thick coating of sawdust he had intended to sluice off in the creek after his coffee.

It was difficult and he was still struggling to get one arm through a sleeve when Pardoe swung down stiffly from his mount, walked across and held the shirt so Clinton could guide his left arm into the dangling, twisted sleeve.

'There you go, young feller,' Pardoe said, panting a little. 'Be better you wash-up though before puttin' it on over all that sawdust. Gonna itch like hell. Why don't you do that while I see Yuma — he up to the house, Blue?'

'Yeah — workin' out how many cows he can run on the Bench . . . '

'A goodly lot, I'd say,' Pardoe answered but he was looking at Clinton who was still only half into the shirt.

'You surely will itch, you don't wash-up first, mister. 'Sides, I've already seen that nasty scar on your left shoulder, so no need to try to cover it up.'

Clinton looked into the old face — which told him nothing. 'Sharps Big Fifty — at extreme range — accident on the Llano Estacado, some years back when I was huntin' buff.'

'Hmmmm — your luck was in that day. Heard of another feller that a similar thing happened to, it was a Sharps, too, blew him about ten feet outta his saddle. Young, frisky fast gun, what was his name now . . . ? Wade, Wayne, somethin' like that. Ever hear about it?'

'Can't say I have.' Clinton's voice was flat. He was standing straight and stiff, eyes flicking to the low branch where his sixgun rig was hanging.

'Don't really matter, he was on the run, anyways.' Pardoe shook his head slowly. 'Musta been tougher'n a grizzly. Got clean away, leavin' a lotta blood behind — ' He suddenly snapped his fingers. 'Yeah! Got it now — *Wade* was the name. Knew his old man some, 'Hard-Luck' Wade, they called him — bit of a boozer, couldn't hold a job. Was gonna put him in a cell for the night once, out on a high trail, him staggerin', hadn't et in a week, by the look of him, when my old hoss went off the edge of a cliff, left me danglin' by my fingernails, hundred feet up. Drunk as he was he hauled me back. Saved my life.' He chuckled. 'Because of him, I broke my law oath, quite a few times where he was concerned. Never did arrest him for nothin' — if he was in my town usually found him a warm cell in the winter. Died years ago. Heard he had a son somewhere, but never met him . . .'

Clinton was aware Blue and Yuma, who had strolled up, were looking at him tensely. He shrugged out of his shirt and rubbed some of the sawdust from his torso. 'Reckon I'll take your advice, Sheriff, and wash-up before I put this shirt on.'

'Sure, son, you do that — I'll likely be gone by the time you get back. Figured I'd best check you out.' Old grey eyes were steady now. 'Well, I have and I got no one on my Wanted list named Clinton, so hope you like it here, son — Yuma's a good man.'

He put out a gnarled right hand and Clinton hesitated only a moment before shaking. 'Obliged, Sheriff.'

Pardoe grunted and turned to Yuma. 'Seems a nice enough feller. Your man Pres did his best to stir things up, figured there was a bounty on Clinton's head and wanted me to check it out . . . You wouldn't have a slug of whiskey to put in that cup of coffee you're gonna offer me, would you, Yuma . . . ? Before I head back to town.'

The rancher smiled. 'Reckon I might find one, come inside and we'll see.'

At the top of the porch steps, Pardoe turned and he could just see Clinton kneeling at the creek's edge, sluicing water over his torso.

'Must've been one *helluva* wound that,' he opined and then followed Yuma inside. 'Be a surefire identifyin' mark on any outlaw — if you got him to take his shirt off.'

Yuma looked carefully at the old sheriff. 'Lucky for Clinton he ain't wanted, then, eh?'

'Well, I guess any man deserves a little luck.'

Yuma figured that was a good enough place to leave it, brought out the bottle of whiskey and watched the light brighten in Pardoe's eyes as he tilted it over the man's mug.

★　★　★

Pres Barnes almost jumped clear out of his skin when Pardoe's quiet voice behind him said, 'What the hell you think you're doin', boy?'

Pres whirled almost falling, knocking down the pile of ragged Wanted dodgers he had placed on Pardoe's desk.

110

'I-I was lookin' through your dodgers. For someone who answered Clinton's description.'

His voice trembled but by the time he finished his heart rate was settling back to normal and he even glared at Pardoe.

'And what did you find? While you're answerin', pick up them dodgers and get your ass off my desk.'

Pres coloured at the sheriff's cold order but obeyed. 'Listen — I still say 'Wade' is part of Clinton's real name.' He shook a dodger he was holding in his right hand. 'From Ridgeback County, Texas. Feller only known as Wade sent to the Pen for ten years for proddin' a rancher's son into goin' for his gun. Don't sound too much like Clinton — till you get to identifyin' marks — ' He rapped his fingernails hard against the stiff dodger. 'Mentions an old shoulder wound — ' He looked smug as he straightened and said, 'Clinton's got a big scar on his shoulder.'

Pardoe began to fill his old pipe from

the recently filled humidor. He nodded. 'Saw it. Caught him out at the Bench without his shirt. Mighty lucky the cougar never chewed his arm off.'

'Cougar! What cougar . . . ?'

'Din' he tell you he was ridin' under a ledge someplace and this cougar someone'd gutshot and left it to die, dropped on him and tried to make a meal outta him?' Pardoe shook his head admiringly. 'Reckon I'd've died of fright but he managed to fight it off, takes real guts that.'

'Listen.' Pres read aloud from the dodger, his mouth dry. 'Wound made by duly sworn-in posse member Hiram 'Bison' Trenton, buffalo hunter, using a '78 Model Sharps Big Fifty . . . '

'I seen enough gunshot wounds to fill a book thick as a Bible, boy — I'm tellin' you, a Sharps Big Fifty would've torn a man's arm clean off. No, that was a cougar, all right.'

'You're makin' that up! No big cat made that wound.'

Pardoe smiled that smile that wasn't

a smile, more of a smirk, spent a little time getting his pipe going. He blew smoke into Pres's face, making the man step back and cough. 'I'm sayin' it and it's a lo-ooong time since anyone called me a liar, boy — '

Pres jumped, blood draining from his face. 'Hell! I weren't doin' that, Tom, honest! I just meant . . . '

'I know, boy, I know. You're all a'tremble at the size of the bounty offered for this 'Wade's' capture, ain't you . . . ?'

'Well — ten thousand bucks! *Dead or Alive*!'

'The rancher's puttin' that up, not the County.'

'Well, don't matter whose payin', that's what it is!'

'Got you all excited, eh? Might sober you up some if you figure out just how you'd go about gettin' that re-ward — I mean, this 'Wade's' s'posed to be lightnin' on the draw, had more gunfights than you've had feeds an' walked away from every one . . . Take

113

more of a man than you'll ever be to claim that reward, boy. Now put them dodgers back in the cupboard where they belong and git.' He blew another plume of smoke in Pres's direction, and his voice hardened. 'I'm sick of the sight of you.'

Pres didn't say another word, but when he left the law office and stomped towards the hitchrail where his horse waited patiently, he was seething.

The horse squealed as its head was wrenched around violently and the spur rowels tore at its flanks as Pres galloped the mount recklessly out of town.

7

Bullets

Yuma walked across the yard to where Clinton was standing by the corrals, one boot on a bottom rail, smoking.

'Comin' along OK,' the rancher opined, indicating the barn.

The doors had been swung now and fitted tolerably well — *good* for barn doors — and the roof had had the last section of shingles laid. Clinton had done this as Blue didn't care much for heights and was plagued by rheumatism.

'Just needs a lick of paint now.'

'Yeah — well, we'll just do the doors, I reckon. Can't run to doin' the whole she-bang.' Yuma had rolled a cigarette and lit up, looking steadily at Clinton. 'Tom Pardoe seems to've known your pa, eh?'

'You could figure it that way — I dunno, mebbe it was Pa rescued him — dunno why he'd say so if it wasn't.'

'Either way — I reckon you were lucky.' Vern nodded, wondering why the sheriff had given him a break, too. 'Just to make sure, got a chore for you out on the range where it's a mite more lonesome: want you to round-up some cattle — OK?

'Name any ranch chore and I've done it, from tick-dipping to castrating.'

'There're some mavericks I've had my eye on,' Yuma said slowly, looking hard.

'Bracken's stock?' Clinton asked with feigned innocence.

Yuma nodded, winking. 'Mavericks belong to anybody who can round 'em up and burn his brand on 'em. You know that.'

'Yeah, law of the range. My guess'd be Bracken let 'em roam the Bench when it was still open range — now you've closed it off and some of his mavericks are still here.'

'Happens young Pres found a bunch of 'em in a blind canyon I'll tell you about. He wanted a bonus before he'd say where it was, but I told him it was all part of his job — I'd've slipped somethin' extra in his pay but he's made a career outta nubbin' folk the wrong way, that boy. Anyways, you care to bring 'em in? Take your time, couple days or so. Me and Blue'll have a brush fence built across that draw under the ledge by then, ready to brand 'em with a Flyin' Y.'

'Sure, don't matter if it takes a couple or three trips, will it?'

'Dunno that there's that many, but no, it won't matter. Just do it in your own time.'

He was obliged to Yuma for his thoughtfulness in giving him a chance to get away from the immediate ranch surroundings. No knowing just what lies Pres Barnes would spread around, being the vindictive cuss he was.

★　★　★

117

Morgan Bragg saw Pres coming, half-hiding on his approach to the Cross Iron main gate. Bragg rode out from behind his tree, rifle butt resting on his thick thigh, finger on the trigger, thumb on the hammer spur.

Pres reined down sharply — for a moment it looked like he would turn tail and make a run for it, but then he saw Jace Vermont between him and the gate, also with a rifle out.

Bragg's laugh halted him. 'Don't run off, kid — you can't outrun a bullet, anyways.'

'Hey, easy, Morg! I-I ain't here for trouble — Yuma done fired me and I need to see Luke.'

'We ain't hirin',' growled Jace, a laconic rangy man.

'Well — I have to see him anyways. Not only about a job.'

'There won't *be* no job!' Bragg growled. 'If that's all you're after, mebbe you best ride off with your tail between your legs while your hide's all in one piece.'

Pres coloured. 'No need for that!

Anyways, I ain't scared of you, Morg, big as you are . . . nor you, Jace.'

Vermont spat and Bragg laughed. 'Bet I could make you scared of me.'

The rifle swung down and Pres stiffened in the saddle. 'Aw, come on, Morg! I-I got a deal to put to Luke! I swear he'll kick your butt you keep me from tellin' him about it.'

Morg's cruel eyes narrowed. 'Any butt-kickin' done around here, I'll do it!'

'With a little help from his friends.' Jace grinned, showing his buck teeth.

Inwardly trembling, Pres made an effort to keep his voice steady. 'I mean it, Morg! This is real important! Could even get The Bench back for Luke.'

Bragg frowned, staring coldly at the nervous kid.

'Aaaalllll right! But I get a tongue-whippin' or worse from Luke and you best book a plot on Boot Hill, you sneerin' little sum'bitch. Watch the gate, Jace, while I take him up to see the boss. An' keep your hands on the saddlehorn, Pres! Git goin' . . .'

Pres didn't really want to talk in front of Bragg but Luke Bracken, irritable and impatient, snapped like an alligator: 'You got somethin' to say, say it! Or get out — I got better things to do with my time than wait till you're ready to tell me whatever it is . . . by the look of you, I'd say Yuma fired you. Well, there ain't no job for you here so you can save your breath.'

Pres was nervous: he hadn't expected to find Bracken in such a foul mood and Morg Bragg, sniggering quietly in the background, just awaiting the word from his boss to start kicking the hell out of him. Pres licked his lips. 'I can get rid of that Clinton for you!' he burst out.

Bragg grunted sardonically. The rancher lifted his hooded eyes and stared. 'You can, huh?'

'Yeah.' Pres swallowed and said quickly. 'It'll cost you five thousand dollars, but . . . '

'Get this blamed idiot outta my sight!' growled Bracken to Bragg and went back

120

to working over his tally books.

Pres heard Bragg move behind him and darted to the side. 'Wait! Wait up! You ain't heard it all yet . . . '

'*Get him the hell outta here!*'

Bragg, cursing, lunged forward, caught Pres as he darted towards the door and slammed him back against the wall, hard enough to jar loose a framed picture. Glass shattered and brought another glare from Bracken. Morg, angry with himself now, fisted up Pres's shirt and slapped him back and forth across the face with one of his big, hard-knuckled hands.

They were brutal, blurring blows and Pres' knees sagged as blood streaked across his cheeks and flowed from a cut lip over his chin. Bragg dragged him towards the door, tearing Pres's shirt, the man's legs stumbling under him. He fell to his knees and Morg lifted a fist to smash down into his battered face and Pres literally screamed:

'I know who he is!'

Morg Bragg had the door open and was about to hurl Pres bodily through when Bracken said,

'Hold up — What d'you mean, you know who he is?'

Pres was still on his knees, fumbled off his neckerchief and dabbed at his battered mouth and bleeding nostrils.

'He escaped from the rockpile somewhere in Texas and there's ten thousand bucks reward . . . '

'Hogwash!' growled Bragg. 'The hell did he do to have that much bounty on his head . . . ?'

'He killed the son of some rich rancher named Ballard — rancher got him railroaded to the Pen for ten years. Now he's escaped — an' Ballard's puttin' up that big bounty, *dead or alive* — Pardoe rode out to check him an' I think he knows who he is — but he's givin' him a break for some reason.'

Bracken waved that away. 'Forget old Tom — tell me more about this ten thousand bucks — and it better be gospel, or I'll have Morg go to work on you with a castratin' knife.'

He didn't need that extra threat: Pres

was scared enough already to tell all he knew. And he did — twice having his head battered by Bragg when he got too excited and garbled his information. When he had finished, he sat on the floor, gasping, dabbing at his blood-smeared face.

'I-I know Yuma's after some mavericks I told him about. He was askin' all about 'em before he fired me. He'll send Clinton up there for sure. I-I could nail him easy.'

'Back-shoot him, you mean,' growled Bragg and Pres didn't deny it.

'Well — I was gonna get him, then I figured we could wire this rancher, Ballard, and tell him we was claimin' the bounty — and split fifty-fifty, Luke.'

'Now ain't that generous of him, eh, boss?'

Bracken was watching Pres with narrowed eyes. 'Got it all worked out, huh? And what about these mavericks? *My own damn cows!* They have to be!' He swore. 'Yuma not only steals my linecamp, now I'm helpin' the sonuver stock his range!'

'With — with Clinton gone, there'll only be Yuma and Blue,' Pres said. 'You — you'll get your mavericks back: won't be no trouble to handle them two — I'll even do it for you.'

'And you an' me get five thousand apiece,' Bracken said, sounding mildly amused.

'Pretty good, huh, Luke?'

'Uh-huh — but why bring me into it at all?'

'I — know I can get at Clinton best from that place you call Bellybuster, right above the canyon where the mavericks've been feedin' and hidin' out. It's on your land and I din' wanta have one of your boys come along and kick me off or worse before I nailed Clinton . . . 'Sides, you're better at words than me — for sendin' the wire to Ballard and claimin' the reward, you know . . . ? He'll take more notice of you, too, you being a bigtime rancher up here.'

Luke Bracken stared at him, his face

blank for a long moment. Then he smiled crookedly. 'You ain't so smart, kid — you've told me all I need to know: where the mavericks are, who's puttin' up the reward — what do I need you for?'

Pres went very still, the blood draining from his face, making the bruises and swelling show up more plainly.

'I-I — Aw, now, Luke, I'm playin' square with you!'

'You're scared witless is what you are,' the rancher told him coldly. 'That's why you come to me in the first place — but you have every right to be scared! — Morg!'

The big ramrod's thick lips moved in a crooked smile, hand moving to his gun butt.

'No!' Pres was in a panic, still on his knees. He threw himself sideways, reaching for his sixgun — but far too nervous to co-ordinate his movements. He fumbled the draw and by that time, Bragg's Colt was filling the office with smoke and thunder. The bullets sent Pres's jerking body sliding across the floor as they slammed home.

'Don't let him bleed on that new rug, dammit!' roared Bracken rising quickly to his feet. 'Jesus Christ! Drag him into the damn corner where there's only floor boards under him — aaah, that's better.'

Bragg looked up, Colt holstered again now. 'What'll we do with him?'

Satisfied that Pres's blood wasn't going to stain the new floor rug, Bracken looked up at Bragg and smiled slowly.

'Why don't we just give him back to Yuma . . . ?'

★   ★   ★

Vern Clinton found the blind canyon where the mavericks were feeding, tore up a dozen bushes and set them across the narrow entrance. The grazing cattle — about two dozen, he figured — just went on nibbling at the sweet-grass, only three bothering to glance towards him.

Those bushes would hold them for now, and while they filled their bellies, he'd fell a few saplings for a drop-gate across a small draw Yuma had told him about. It would hold six or eight comfortably, a good manageable size for him to drive down to where Yuma and Blue waited — then return for another bunch.

Clinton enjoyed this ranch work. He had, many times over the years, thought of trying to settle down on his own small spread, but there was always someone to pick an argument with him and it inevitably ended in a gunfight . . . and he had to ride out. No point in sticking around where other eager challengers could find him . . .

He didn't mind losing a little sweat — not even in the bottom of the sawpit, except for the itching dust, though he wouldn't admit that out loud.

Maybe it really was time he hung up his gun.

Right now it was no problem to cut down four tall, slim saplings, trim them so they fitted across the entrance, and slotted more or less neatly into the rocks. The draw was deep enough to give him time to get the saplings in place while the mavericks would be sorting themselves out after he drove them in, checking the graze potential — which they would do, immediately.

He placed the saplings, two a side, in convenient positions, then went back to the blind canyon for the first of the mavericks — he figured to try six, for a start.

Instead, he found a dead man draped over the line of brush he had set-up across the narrow canyon entrance earlier. The figure was bloody — and very dead.

Pres Barnes.

This information flashed through Clinton's mind and before it had been fully realized, he was diving out of the saddle, snatching his rifle from the scabbard, deliberately kicking the mount so it would run off.

As it swerved, whinnying, the first rifle opened up, raking the place where he had sat the horse a few moments earlier. A bullet clipped the saddle horn, sending the horse weaving wildly, whickering in alarm and naked fear as the slug ricocheted.

Clinton rolled behind a rock, kicked and squirmed to give his body as much protection as possible. He raked his alert gaze around the slopes — those bullets had come from higher ground.

He saw the gunsmoke all right but they had him pinned — there was one man almost in a direct line with him now, halfway up the slope overlooking the canyon, and a second one, slightly higher, off to the right.

He ducked as lead hammered his rock. So far he had no target. He could waste a couple of shots by shooting under the pall of gunsmoke, hoping it would startle one of the men into showing himself, but over many years, Clinton had found it was best to conserve ammunition — that last bullet had literally been a life-saver more than once in the past.

The second man up there made a mistake: probably not used to holding position while he pinned down his target. More than likely he was impatient to nail who he was shooting out — and he grew careless.

He moved fast, but hunched over, legs bent. His body showed above the rocks and Clinton's rifle leapt to his shoulder and the crash of his shot drowned one from the other man, now settled in lower down. He ducked back, and between two rocks saw the running man blown on to his side. He was hit, and probably badly, but that strong instinct for self-preservation that all men had, allowed him to find strength to rear up enough and throw himself headlong for another rock.

It was only a short lunge — three, maybe four feet at the outside — and his body was still airborne when Clinton's next slug dropped him in mid-flight. The rifle fell, clattered and skidded down the slope, fired when the hammer spur struck something solid at the bottom.

The weapon leapt wildly and Clinton glimpsed a puff of rock dust from the small ridge that held the first man. It must have been close — maybe even winged him — for he stifled a yell and heaved up and over a low rim of shale, his diving body just a blur.

Still, Clinton recognized him: Morgan Bragg, a Cross Iron man, who had been pointed out to him by Blue when he was showing Clinton the boundaries of Yuma's Flying Y.

'Meanest sonuver in the County,' Blue had said. 'Big man, big fists, and likes to use 'em to smash a man up, big or small. Stay clear of him, Vern.'

Sounded like good advice to Clinton, but now it was well past the 'staying clear' stage. He was Bragg's target — but, just to even things up, Bragg was *his* target, too.

Bragg got in the first shot, as Clinton

moved so as to get room to place his gun barrel between the rocks. Morg's lead hit the brim of Clinton's hat, spurting dust, burning across his scalp, mostly on the left side.

He dropped flat, breathless, warm blood oozing, bright pinpoints of light whirling behind his eyes as he realized how close he had come to having his head blown off.

But Bragg had miscounted or had a breech stoppage.

While he tried to free the action, straining at the lever, Clinton wiped off some blood, took cool aim and shot Bragg through the head.

Morg dropped, his thick body jamming in the crevice beneath his hiding place.

Not that it mattered: there was no spark of life left in him.

But the other man, Jace Vermont, who had taken one of Clinton's bullets through the body, groaned aloud and called feebly, one bloody hand half raised: 'Help . . . me . . . '

Clinton waited, dizzy, head throbbing, and the man cried out again, even more plaintively. Still Clinton waited — the pain in the cries sounded genuine but many of these hardcases were pretty good actors when it came to feigning hurt.

There was a movement over there and he saw Jace slump forward between the rocks, arms dangling limply.

Good enough — he couldn't reach a gun from that position before Clinton put another bullet into him. So, Clinton stood slowly, started a cautious circuitous approach, and was closing in, by now convinced Vermont was really hit bad, when there was a shot from high up on the ridge.

Flatter. Cut short. *Carbine*, his mind registered even as he dropped, the bullet snarling past his left ear.

Dammit! Three of them! Bracken must really want to make sure of him . . .

Then, a new voice startled him. *A woman's voice!*

'That was just a warning — I've got a bead on your head right now! Just try moving a finger of your hand holding that gun if you want me to prove it to you. Otherwise, stand slowly, hands raised, but leave your rifle where it is!'

Clinton slowly released his grip on the rifle and climbed warily to his feet, every nerve end feeling like it was being drawn through his skin.

He straightened — *still breathing!* — and lifted his hands shoulder-high.

'Just take it easy, ma'am, whoever you are! I know when I'm on the wrong end of a gun.'

'Not for long, because I'm going to kill you, anyway, and I want to look into your eyes while I do it.'

Then what've I got to lose? he thought as she stepped out from behind a rock, carbine braced into her hip. She wore a blue-and-white checkered shirt, corduroy trousers tucked into plain half-boot tops — high-heeled but no spurs.

There was a lot of wavy brown hair showing beneath a flat-crowned, narrow-brimmed hat held on with a thong under a strong jaw. Her face was softly feminine, but not of heart-stopping beauty. He reckoned she was in her early twenties . . . The eyes were a startling pale grey and looked mighty damn icy now as she started forward, watching him all the time.

She should have spared a glance or two for where she was walking: one of her boots rolled on a half-buried pebble that gave way underfoot. She instinctively threw out an arm for balance, thereby swinging the carbine well off line.

She screamed quite loudly when his Colt blasted, the first bullet snarling away from the rock at head-height, the second kicking sand over her boots. She staggered, and by that time he was within arm's reach and yanked the carbine from her grip. It went off but the barrel was angled well away from them both. He tossed it over a clump of boulders and stepped back, jerking up his smoking gun barrel.

She was half-crouched now, glaring, but with a touch of fear beneath the anger: face white as a starched table napkin, her eyes seeming to almost smoulder — like banked coals flickering into life.

Her voice was shaky. 'My God! — I never believed them when they said how fast you were with a gun!'

'Got a stiff arm today,' he told her wryly and then genuine anger blazed at him. It faded some as he added, 'Otherwise you'd be dead. Now, just who the hell are you?'

8

Amy

Her name was Amy Stokes.

She said it slowly with a strange look on her face, her eyes half-hooded, watching him closely. *Expecting a reaction . . .?* The name meant nothing to him.

They were on a flat ledge above the dead men — Jace Vermont had lived long enough to tell Clinton that Morgan Bragg had killed Pres. It was Bracken's idea to bring the body to Banjo Canyon where Clinton was gathering the mavericks. Bragg and Jace were to kill Clinton and make it look like he and Pres had shot it out. Pres being a grudge-holder and hating Clinton anyway, it would seem logical enough. But Clinton had proved too good for them . . .

'Why do you want to kill me?' he asked the girl now. She tilted her jaw and looked coldly at him. 'Because you killed my father.'

He frowned. 'I don't remember anyone named 'Stokes'.'

'That doesn't surprise me! I wouldn't think you'd be the kind who'd remember the names of men you've killed! Perhaps, 'Notch Six' or 'Seven', or *larger*! Something like that would be near enough for you — but not names!'

'I don't notch my guns. Who was your father? Did I know him or was he just someone who happened along and figured he could beat me to the draw?'

'Oh! How I *despise* you!' She clenched her small fists and stamped a foot. He dabbed at his still-bleeding scalp with a folded neckerchief. 'My father taught you how to be a gunfighter! And you turned on him and killed him!'

Clinton stiffened and stared back in shocked silence. She curled a lip disdainfully. 'You — You're talking about Rapido?'

'Of course I'm talking about Rapido! He was my father and I loved him and . . . '

'You would've been only a shaver when it happened! No more'n what? Nine or ten, maybe . . . ?'

'I had just turned eleven when we got the news how you'd not only gotten him drunk, but called him out after a stagecoach accident that left him injured and groggy and not in full command of himself!'

That damn stage driver! Embellished the incident so he could keep the free drinks flowing . . . God-damn!

'That's not how it happened.'

'Naturally, you'd claim that!'

'Shut up a minute and I'll tell you — Shut up! I said!' This last when she tried to interrupt. His head was throbbing and this new problem didn't help. 'Now you sit there and listen, miss. You damn well listen!'

He told her about the bank raid and all the celebratory drinking, then the stage wreck and Rapido's surge of violent anger. 'His bouts of hard drinking were becoming more and more frequent, more — unreasoning.' He kept talking as she tried to interrupt. 'He'd had a headwound a doctor told him could cause him to go crazy with the pain sometimes — it was aggravated by booze — and he'd swallowed a helluva lot by the time that stage was wrecked.'

'And which you took advantage of!'

He held up a hand. 'He'd always drummed into me over and over until I was sick of hearing him yell '*Draw!*' any time, day or night, that I had to *do it*! I had to draw on command — instantly! If I didn't, he'd belt me. When he called 'Draw!' at the stage wreck . . . ' He shrugged. 'I just reacted automatically.'

She almost spat in her disbelief.

'That's how it happened, no matter what that damn Jinglebob says. But all the time I knew him, Rapido never once mentioned a wife — or daughter.'

'Of course not. He kept us separate to the life he led. None of us were

140

proud that he was an outlaw and he only came to see us at long intervals. But he did love us. And we, him . . . He looked after us as well as he could.'

Clinton nodded slightly. There *had* been several times over the months he had ridden with Rapido when the man had disappeared for a week or so and said nothing about where he had been upon his return. The last, only weeks before the bank robbery, was when he really started hitting the booze. *Had something happened on that visit . . . ?*

All of the gang had been surprised when he suggested robbing that bank: it was widely-known to be well-protected — he'd said — *yes!* — he'd said something like, 'I need a decent stake *now!* There's others to think about besides me . . . ' It could mean anything, but in the light of what Amy was saying — it sounded like he wanted to make sure she and her mother were provided for. Now that was a term that tightened his belly: *provided for*, as if Rapido figured he mightn't be around to see to it personally . . .

Amy's thoughts were obviously far away, too, remembering, he supposed, and he asked quietly enough, 'Where were you and your mother living?'

'Bodkin Creek — That's . . . '

'Yeah, I know — Ballard County, Texas!'

She smiled coldly, told him that when she was eighteen, she, like everyone else in Ballard County, had heard about his gunfight with Gavin Ballard.

'No one liked Gavin much but when I found out it was you who had killed him, I stole a gun from the rancher Ma and I were working for and went looking for you. By then you were in jail. Both my mother and I were disappointed when they broke up the lynch party but we celebrated after your trial when the judge sentenced you to ten years on the rockpile. We were willing to accept that as fitting punishment — because we'd know where you were and the day they finally released you, I'd be waiting.'

He shook his head slowly. 'You sure do hate hard!'

'I told you — I loved my father — and he loved me! *And* my mother.' There was a break in her voice as she said this, almost belligerently, and the gleam of tears which she brushed away irritably with the back of one small, tanned hand.

'Don't go loco now, but — was Rapido married to your ma?'

Her jaw quivered. 'He — they weren't — *properly* married, but he took good care of us and . . . '

'Amy — I'm telling you the truth. I didn't want to kill Rapido! Hell, I looked on him almost as my father.'

She leapt up, eyes blazing. 'How dare you! Don't — don't you ever say that again!'

He held up a hand. 'Easy now! Listen, how did he talk about me when he came to visit? That's if he mentioned me at all . . . '

She was silent and there was a small, tight frown between her eyes and he had the feeling she was having some kind of inner struggle. Then her resolve obviously hardened as she looked at him soberly and said, reluctantly,

'You were — mentioned — and — well, he did seem to feel well-disposed towards you! That's what makes it so despicable that you killed him, just to prove how fast you were with a gun! After he had treated you so well.'

Clinton nodded gently. 'I can see how you might think that. Look, Amy, I can't prove I'm telling the truth, not unless I find that stage driver and by now his brain is so pickled with liquor he wouldn't know the truth if it jumped up and bit him on the ass. Pardon my language.'

'I'll pardon you nothing!'

He sighed, spread his hands. 'OK — then it's a stand-off. You come with me when I take in the bodies, meet Yuma and Blue, and then have a talk with Tom Pardoe . . . '

'Pardoe? He's sheriff of this county?'

'Yeah — why?'

'He's a famous old lawman — Rapido was his deputy once, a long time ago. He always spoke well of Pardoe. They had some kind of a — a deal, I suppose you'd call it. That Rapido and his gang never operated in Pardoe's territory. That way, they could remain friends. He thought a lot of Tom Pardoe. I don't recall ever meeting him but I'll ride in with you. Just don't expect me to do you any favours. I'll tell what I saw — truthfully — but that's all.'

'Good enough.'

At least, for the moment, she seemed to have lost her urge to kill him — likely just put it on the hob to simmer to be reviewed later.

Maybe that was some kind of progress, though.

Maybe.

★   ★   ★

Amy was more confused than she wanted to let on.

Yuma Hardy and Blue McElroy had both made it clear that they thought Clinton was a man to ride the river with, as they said in the part of Texas where she lived. It was the highest compliment a man could be paid — and not earned easily.

But she knew what she knew! There was no escaping the fact that he had killed her father! And that account had yet to be settled.

Then Pardoe had confused her further by his attitude.

'There's a lot of good men with a bad streak in 'em, missy, and a few bad men with a good streak, your pa was one.' Pardoe jerked a thumb casually at Clinton. 'He's another. Your pa recognized it in him, I guess, and — well, I owe my life to this man's father . . . Good runs in the blood just as they claim bad does.'

'I know nothing good about him!'

Pardoe gave Clinton a wink at her primness. 'Guess not, but you're kinda one-eyed in this, you have to admit.'

'I admit nothing.'

'Feisty, ain't she? Missy, I been a lawman for forty years. Thirty-some of them I went by the book, my fists and my gun — I took the law to wherever it was needed, and I rammed it down folk's throats — and seen the way they looked at me when I passed 'em in the street.' He scratched at his greying hair, shook his head slightly. 'I never felt good about it, knowing folk not only were scared of me — they hated me, too. So, I made a decision I've never regretted, though I lost a lot of sleep over it at first. I decided to bend the law here and there where it didn't *need* to be hammered home with a bullet. I'd become such a miserable cuss I never even stopped when I knocked a stick of sugar candy out of a little gal's hands when I was in a hurry to git out of the store to get to a drunk I saw on the boardwalk through the window. I heard her cryin' but I ignored her and threw that drunk in a cell. Woke in the middle of the night, winter it was, and damn, if

I didn't take him down an extra blanket.' He shook his head again, wonderingly. 'I slept better after that, found I had an appetite I thought I'd lost forever. Next day I seen the little gal an' bought her a whole bag of candy. Fact is, I went a mite — soft, I guess. I still dished out the law, but a mite more lenient. I've felt heaps better because I'd turned into a human bein', instead of just actin' like some kinda killin' machine.'

She frowned. 'What's this got to do with me?'

'See, missy? I suddenly realized what I just told you about the good and bad streaks in folk — there was *good* good, and there sure was *bad* bad! All a matter of individuals — and just what law they'd breached, of course.'

'Rapido always said you were the kind of lawman the West could do with,' she admitted huskily. 'He respected you.'

Pardoe looked mighty pleased. 'Ol' Rap said that about me? Well, well, well, then mebbe you'll b'lieve me when I say that in my book, this feller here had no other choice than to draw agin your pa. An' just think how fast Rapido was! Hell, it'd take a lotta guts for any man to go up agin that kinda speed.'

'I-I don't care about his — guts!' she said, staring hard at Clinton, though maybe not quite so coldly. 'The fact remains — he killed Rapido.'

'Nothin's ever gonna change that, missy — only the way you see it.'

'There is only *one* way,' she told him coldly.

Pardoe sighed and looked across at Clinton who was frowning slightly at her. 'I gotta watch my back from now on? That what you're saying?' Clinton asked Amy in clipped tones.

'She better not be!' cut in the sheriff before the girl could answer. 'I'll treat it as murder if he turns up dead, missy, and you're anywheres around . . . You won't find me bein' so soft about the law then, neither.'

She was pale but obstinate, stood

abruptly. 'Can I go now?'

'Leave your carbine,' Pardoe told her as she turned to where the weapon rested across the end of the big desk.

'It's my only means of protection.'

'No — I'm your means of protection. In this town, you feel threatened, come see me, missy, that's why I'm here.'

She curled a lip sardonically. 'After what you've just told me? The way I see it, you apply the law how you see fit.'

'It's my way. Now, you simmer down some and you'll find it's worked well enough for this town and a lot of others. You don't like it, you can always leave.'

'With or without my gun?'

Pardoe shook his head slowly at Clinton. 'Now, I'm tellin' you, *amigo* — you *better* watch your back!'

They both thought they heard the girl laugh softly as she left the law office, pleased she had upset them both.

'Stubborn as all get-out,' Clinton said, looking at his blood on the neckerchief, raising it to the scalp again.

'Dangerous,' was the sheriff's only comment.

'Yeah. About these dead men . . . am I off the hook?'

'Was never on it — thanks to the gal, tellin' what she saw.' He seemed puzzled. 'She's doin' this because she thinks she has to, not because she wants to.'

'Could've fooled me. Dammit, Tom, I don't want to have to kill her!'

Pardoe gave him as steady a glance as he could with his rheumy old eyes. 'Might not have to, if she gets in first shot.'

Clinton heaved a sigh. 'Just what I wanted to hear! Looks like I'll have to move on.'

'She'll follow.'

'Dammit! I like it here. Yuma and Blue, you, giving me a break — it's the kinda spot I've looked for for years, even before that damn Ballard kid prodded me.'

'Stay — Yuma needs you. He's the one gave you the real break.'

Clinton was silent, took out tobacco and papers and made a cigarette. When he lit-up, he exhaled smoke and nodded.

'There's still Bracken, Yuma's tough, but he tends to fight by the rules — like filing on Big Cat Bench and so on — I guess I owe him, all right.'

Pardoe made no comment, toyed with his battered old pipe.

'You going to see Bracken about Pres?'

Pardoe sighed. 'I'd better — Jace Vermont's word won't count for much but mebbe the gal'd side you as a witness to what he said, mebbe not — I wouldn't count on it, not if she figured it'd make trouble for you if she kept quiet. I doubt I'll throw a scare into Bracken, but I'll try.'

'Just keep him off Yuma's neck, that's the main thing. I can handle whatever he throws at me.'

Pardoe sighed. 'You better let the sawbones take a look at that wound. Must be deeper'n you thought.' Clinton nodded: wincing, as Pardoe began to pack his pipe bowl. 'Could be this town, and the range out there, is gonna see some excitin' times pretty damn soon.'

Excitement was the one thing Clinton could do without right now.

He'd had enough of that over the years, was lucky to be still alive, and he knew it . . . Ballard, his hardcases, and Bracken, he could handle — but Amy Stokes . . . ?

Too bad she wasn't a man. Then it could all be over in an eye-blink.

Just as long as it took him to draw and shoot.

9

You're a Liar!

'Met up with your father a few times after he pulled me back from that cliff,' Pardoe said suddenly, into a long silence that had formed between himself and Clinton while they smoked.

His words brought Clinton's head up fast. 'Where'd it happen?'

'Out on the Palo Duro, heyday of the buffalo hunters — I was after some squaw-killer, found him in a runners' camp but it came down to guns. So I was ridin' lonesome on that cliff trail when my hoss, winged in the shootout, stepped over the edge. Lucky for me Hard-Luck was just comin' round after a bout with the bottle, was tryin' to find his way back home, a sorry mess. You mind me talkin' about him like that?'

'Hell, it's the only way I knew him.

Funny, he told me a few times he was a real-life hero, he'd saved a man from going over a cliff. No names or anything — I never knew whether to believe him or not.'

'It was true enough. Odd times I met up with him I tried to straighten him out but never did succeed in gettin' him real sober, saw it was no use. So, when I could, I just kept an eye on him, slipped him a few dollars.' Pardoe re-lit his pipe that had gone out. 'Knew it'd go on booze and not grub, but — well, you know. Years later, I heard how his kid shot and killed the gambler who fleeced him and had him beat-up. Always wanted to meet you. Now I have.'

'I'm glad of it. You've given me the break I need. I aim to make the most of it, Tom, try to get some sort of normal life here.'

'Well, you got your chance. But you gotta stay within the law, you savvy that?'

'Sure.' Clinton said it warily.

Pardoe suddenly grinned. 'My kinda

law, that is — not *exactly* by the book these days . . . '

The street door crashed back against the wall and both men reacted: Pardoe froze with his pipe halfway to his mouth; Clinton was on his feet, crouched, hand on gunbutt, facing the big figure standing in belligerent silhouette against the sunlit street.

'Judas, you move fast all right, gunslinger!' It was Luke Bracken's deep voice and he stepped into the office, leaving the door swinging on strained hinges. 'I'm impressed.'

The rancher let his hard gaze pass across Clinton who was relaxing now, and set it on Pardoe. 'My wrangler seen 'em bring in Morg Bragg and Jace to the undertaker's — what I hear, you killed my men, gunslinger.'

'And Bragg killed Pres Barnes, your wrangler mention him, too?'

'Yeah, he said Pres was there. But Bragg never killed him.' Bracken looked squarely, openly, at the sheriff. 'This sonuver's tryin' to make trouble for me,

Tom, likely put up to it by Yuma.'

'Jace lived long enough to tell us Bragg shot Pres on Cross Iron, said you told 'em to take the body to Banjo Canyon, bushwhack me, and set it up to look like Pres and I'd shot it out.'

'Sounds like you could've . . . Pres had no likin' for you,' Bracken said easily. 'And he was a mean sonuver — I know damn well Morg never shot him on Cross Iron.'

'There's a witness to Jace's confession, Luke,' Pardoe said easily. 'Young woman named Amy Stokes — she can back-up Vern's story.'

'If she's a friend of Clinton's it's only natural she would.'

Clinton snorted. 'Friend? She's trying to kill me!'

Bracken arched his heavy eyebrows. 'Ah, now, mebbe I better meet this female assassin. But you still can't prove Morg Bragg killed Pres or the rest of it. I'll deny all knowledge of any part of it. Mebbe Morg and Jace figured they were doin' me a favour, settin' it up of their own accord but I know nothin' about it. That's my official statement, Tom — take it or leave it.'

'Mebbe you're lying.'

Clinton's words fell heavily in the room and even Pardoe sat up straighter in his chair. 'Easy, Vern!'

Bracken stood like a ramrod, eyes narrowed as he glared down at Clinton in his straightback chair. 'I know I'm no match for you with a gun, feller. But you come outside and I'll whale the tar outta you with my fists.'

'Hold it right there!' snapped Pardoe, standing as fast as his rheumatics would allow. 'There'll be no . . .'

He didn't finish what he was saying. Clinton came up out of his chair fast, both hands jabbing the rancher hard in his big chest. Bracken staggered as far as the doorway. Pardoe yelled as Clinton took two long strides and swung a left hook that clipped Bracken on the jaw. It half-turned the stumbling man and he hit the low rail on the landing, flailed his arms wildly before it

158

snapped under his weight.

Bracken landed all asprawl in the street and a buckboard swung wildly to miss him, the driver cursing. As Bracken struggled up, Clinton hurled himself off the landing. His body hit the big rancher full in the chest. They went down, locked together now, rolling and punching and kneeing, raising a dust cloud, soon noticed by folk on the street.

As they finally lumbered to their feet, a crowd formed and started yelling. Neither fighter noticed: their concentration was on each other now, both hatless, clothes dirty, fists up and swinging. Bracken moved his head and let a straight right slip past his left ear, stepped forward, getting one leg between Clinton's.

Clinton staggered back as a punishing tattoo drummed across his chest, dropped lower to his midriff. He sagged in the middle and Bracken curled a lip as he hooked a right into the lower ribs, brought up his knee as Clinton doubled over.

Vern twisted his head and caught

only the side of the rising knee, mostly on his shoulder. It knocked him back, but also out of range, momentarily, of Bracken's fists. The rancher stumbled slightly and Clinton spun to his left, came back looping a haymaker that thudded into the side of Bracken's thick neck. The rancher almost went down but, grunting with effort, wrenched himself back in time to meet Clinton's onslaught.

Arms blurred as they hammered each other, skin tore, blood flowed. Bracken's left eye was already starting to close and Clinton's right took advantage of it, flattening the man's ear on that side. Bracken yelled and reeled, Clinton taking a long step after him, staying within range, hitting the reddening ear again, then hooking into the jaw. Luke's head snapped around and he went down, putting out a hand to keep from falling all the way. Somehow they had worked in close to a hitch rail now and the four horses there began to snort and stomp and whinny. Bracken grabbed Clinton's shirt and pulled him in close, rolling so that the gunfighter was beneath the stomping hoofs, trying to hold him there.

One grazed Clinton's left leg and he yelled, violently, wrenching his body away. It hurt but his movement threw him on top of the startled rancher and immediately smashed an elbow into Luke's nose. Blood spurted and his grip on Vern loosened.

Clinton flailed free, rolled away from the prancing mounts, kicked Bracken as the man tried to get to hands and knees. The rancher fell back amongst the thudding hoofs and frantically scrabbled to get out of range. He caught two blows across the back but managed to roll out on the far side. Wild-eyed, bloody-faced, he lurched to his feet — just as Clinton dodged between the still tethered horses, reaching for Bracken's shirt.

He got a grip but the cloth ripped. Still, it pulled Bracken off-balance and Clinton managed to hit him in the face with bruised knuckles that skidded across bloody flesh. The rancher shook his head, swung a backhand blow that made Clinton dodge so fast he lost his footing and went down to one knee. Bracken roared as he swung a boot at the other's head. Clinton took the kick on a raised left arm but the force of the blow still stretched him out. Bracken ran at him, boot raised to stomp on his face.

Clinton scooped up a handful of dirt and gravel, flung it at the man as he rolled away. He rose, left arm hanging, numb and useless. When the rancher saw his opponent was virtually one-armed right now, he grinned through split lips, and came bulling in, aiming to end this as quickly and bloodily as he could, big, knotted fists at the ready.

He wasn't very successful. Vern Clinton whipped out his Colt and slammed it across the side of Bracken's head. The man dropped in his tracks, eyes rolling up to show the whites, knocked cold . . .

The crowd were silent for about five seconds and then began yelling, some happy to see the bullying Bracken stretched out in the dust, others calling Clinton names for fighting 'dirty'.

But no one got too abusive, for he was still holding the Colt in his hand, dragging down big breaths, shifting his feet several times so as to stay upright. Pardoe, standing beside the broken landing rail, kept his old face neutral.

'Oughta lock you both up for disturbin' the peace — but seems you fellers have provided some entertainment, so — go get yourselves fixed-up at the doctor's, then stay clear of each other long as you're in town. Fact, you bein' the one still walkin', Vern, you better ride out soon as Doc Burns finishes with you.' His eyes raked the crowd and picked out Cross Iron's wrangler. 'Bronc — you see your boss gets back to Cross Iron — but start one hour after Clinton leaves. You let 'em get together again an' I'll lock you up for a month.'

The wrangler swore he would see Bracken home safely, long after Clinton had left town . . .

Limping towards the boardwalk, left arm still stiff and half-paralysed, dabbing at his bleeding face, Clinton saw Amy Stokes amongst the crowd.

'Enjoy it?'

'No, I wanted the other man to win.'

★   ★   ★

When Bracken came out of the doctor's, helped by Bronc, the wrangler, he had a bandage over his busted nose and one ear, his hat sitting on top precariously. His face was a variety of colours: red from mercurochrome, yellow from iodine, blue-grey from spreading bruises.

His eyes were colourless, dead metal — like looking at the noses of bullets in a Colt's cylinder. They fixed on Amy Stone as she walked across from where she had been looking in the window of a baker's shop.

'Mr Bracken?'

He nodded, slowing, and Bronc, not quite sure what to do, said, 'I'll go get the mounts, boss.'

Bracken waved him away, not taking his eyes off the girl. 'I'm Luke Bracken, Cross Iron spread. You wouldn't be the one wants to kill that son of a bitch Vern Clinton, would you?'

She flushed a little at his tone and the lascivious way he was looking at her. It made her angry so she answered more curtly than was necessary. 'I'm Amy Stokes — and, yes, I have a — problem with Clinton.'

'You and me both. Wanta come out to my ranch? Mebbe we can work out some kind of plan to nail the sonuver . . . stay overnight if you like,' he added with a faint leer.

Amy shook her head. 'I did think I might need some help now that the sheriff is obviously on Clinton's side, but on second thoughts, I'm not so sure. I think you're the bullying type, Mr Bracken, and would want to run things. No, I'm sorry to have troubled you, but I like to work alone.'

'Then be damned to you.' Bracken was in a foul mood with all his aches and pains and the taste of stale blood and he had no patience to bandy words with this woman — good-looking enough but he had no real interest in that side of her either, right now.

'And damn you, too, *Mister* Bracken!' Her eyes blazed and he almost changed his mind and apologized — he liked his women feisty and fighting. But an overwhelming pain slid a knife into his belly and he cursed instead.

It was all Amy needed and she turned sharply, walking away stiffly.

'You need a gun, you know where to come!' he called after her and was surprised to see her hesitate briefly, but then she continued on and turned a corner. '*Bronc!* Where the hell are you . . . ?'

As he and the wrangler rode out of town, Bracken saw the girl again.

She was entering the Telegraph Office next to the stage depot . . .

* * *

Pardoe looked up from the ledger he was writing in as the office door swung back — Bracken had busted the lock with his violent entry and there would need to be a padlock and chain fixed to it until a new lock was attached.

Tom Pardoe thought it might be the handyman from the general store coming to do the job but was surprised to see the haggard visitor was Hank Rollins, from the telegraph office. The man was skinny as a rail, had a prominent Adam's apple which jerked several times as he approached the desk. He was holding one of his yellow, flip-back notebooks, close to his chest. He pushed back his green eyeshade and adjusted his wire-rimmed spectacles.

'Tom — I-I'm about to break the law and I want your word you won't do nothin' about it.'

'That's askin' a lot, Hank, when I dunno what you're gonna do. You want to kill someone? Poison a neighbour's

dog? Hold up the bank, mebbe . . . ?
Any of those things I'm duty-bound to
do somethin'. Now what the blazes are
you so excited about? You look like
you're practisin' for an Indian war-
dance . . . Stand still, man.'

Hank Rollins licked his dry lips and
looked down at his notebook, then held
it out towards the sheriff.

'I-I ain't sent it yet — and showin' it
to you is violatin' federal law: a private
message, you see an' . . . '

'Yeah, yeah, I know the law, Hank,
but — ' Pardoe paused and whistled
softly, lips pursed a long time after the
sound had stopped. 'She's gonna get
that gunfighter one way or another,
ain't she?'

The telegraphist nodded vigorously.
He pointed to the last line with a horny-
nailed finger that trembled slightly.

'See what she says? *Reward not
necessary. Just come quickly.* She wants
Clinton bad, all right.'

'Mmmm — well, she came from
Ballard County so she'd know all about

Clinton gunnin'-down Gavin Ballard. I've confiscated her carbine, see, so she's sendin' for Ballard himself, telling him where to find Vern Clinton.' He glanced up. 'You say you ain't sent this yet . . . ? Maybe best if you don't send it, Hank.'

'Aw, no! I-I can lose my job just showin' this to you, Sheriff, but it's been written down in my record book, which you'll see is the official one from Western Union — I write the message and it's automatically copied through carbon paper on to another leaf. Each page is numbered an' easily checked against my message log . . . '

'All right, all *right*! But, goddammit, Ballard'll arrive here with his own posse, armed to the teeth — Clinton won't stand a chance. And then there's the town! Ballard's a vindictive cuss. If he decides we been hidin'-out Clinton — no tellin' what'll happen.'

Hank's jaw jutted. 'I still gotta send that message, Tom — I've accepted it and it's been paid for and now I gotta send it. Just figured you'd like to know about it.'

'Yeah, well, I'm obliged, Hank. But damn that gal! How come a sweet-lookin' little thing like her can be so damn stiff-necked about killin' a man who's just as upset about what's happened as she is!'

'I dunno, Tom, but I got a feelin' she's gonna get it done any way she can and the hell with the consequences.'

'Yeah,' agreed Pardoe heavily. 'Me, too.'

10

Big Guns

Yuma and Blue stared at Clinton as he dismounted stiffly outside the cabin. They saw the glint of bandages, the bruises and cuts and the way he limped as he off-saddled and threw the rig across the top rail of the corral.

Carrying his rifle and saddle-bags, he made his slow way to the small landing at the front of the building.

'I'll get some coffee on,' Blue said, turning back into the cabin.

'He'll need somethin' stronger'n that,' Yuma reckoned, going inside also.

Clinton dropped into a chair at the deal table, breathing hard.

Blue rummaged in a cupboard and brought out a part-full unlabelled dark green bottle. He held it up. 'Better have it in your coffee — mite strong for that

171

cut mouth. Who gave it to you?'

'Me and Bracken had a small difficulty,' Clinton said.

'Glad it wasn't any bigger,' opined Blue, setting the coffee pot over the fire. 'How come . . . ?'

Clinton told it succinctly. 'My fault for callin' him a liar: still, if he'd called me one I'd've likely shot him.'

'Tom Pardoe woulda loved that. He riled?'

'Sort of — made us leave town at different times. Man, what I wouldn't give for a hot bath up to my armpits, and a young, sympathetic woman to massage my tired muscles.'

'How about Amy Stokes?' grinned Blue.

'Anyone but Amy. Not sure what to do about her. If she gets her hands on a gun, I reckon she'll come after me.'

'Can't convince her you had no choice with her father?'

'Yuma, far as I know there's only one witness still livin' — or maybe not — who knows what happened. Jingle-bob Swain's been getting free drinks for years on the story of that stage crash and the gunfight, twisted outta all proportion! Likely drank himself to death by now.'

'Don't reckon she'll ever see it your way?'

Clinton snorted, savouring the smell of alcohol fumes rising from the coffee now. He sipped and sighed. 'Hits the spot. No, she's too one-eyed.'

'She might just quit the county now Pardoe's warned her,' suggested Yuma and Blue snorted this time. 'No, I mean, anythin' happens to Vern now, she knows she'll be blamed . . . '

Soberly, Vern said, 'Hope Bracken don't realize that.'

★   ★   ★

After almost four days travelling the Western Union Telegraph Wire in various directions, Amy's message finally caught up with Julius Ballard in a town the Mexicans called *A'guapo* — 'Handsome'. It was quite a good-looking town, a mix of clapboard, split-log and adobe. The Mission was impressive, straddling the only high ground around for miles, looking out over the square-grid streets and buildings. Handsome Creek was prone to flooding with the Spring rains and the Mission's large bronze bell — originating in Madrid, Spain — tolled its warning each year as the muddy tide approached, and for other natural disasters.

But Ballard had no eye for architecture or history — the Spanish built the Mission in the late 1600s. His sole interest for years — apart from making money — had been in the man he knew only as 'Wade' — and now, thanks to this Stokes' woman's telegraph message, also as 'Vern Clinton'.

Since it was realized that Wade had somehow escaped, after the train wreck, he hadn't slept more than three or four hours a night. He was off his food and had griping stomach pains and constant indigestion. He let his business interests slide, made many sloppy and indifferent decisions. His partners and associates were on the verge of voting him off the various boards he was involved with, including a new railroad he was backing. But he didn't care.

His only true concern now was in finding Wade and killing the man — he had no intention of bringing him back alive to finish his prison sentence. Before, knowing his son's murderer was dying a little every day on the rockpile in a very tough, high security prison, was acceptable. But the unthinkable had happened: he had escaped and Ballard had immediately thrown all his resources into running down Wade — he wouldn't know real peace now until the man was dead.

It was hard for his partners to accept that a cold-eyed, hard-headed go-getter like Ballard had allowed the death of his arrogant, swaggering son-of-a-bitch of a son to turn him into a mawkish avenger who cared little or nothing for friendships, the law — or his business liabilities.

Some of his associates saw it as a chance to rid themselves once and for all of Ballard's overbearing ways — *see how haughty and high-falutin' he was when the coffers sprung a leak and the source of his power drained away.* There were several cold-eyed men waiting in the wings, eager to take over Ballard's *Lone Star Consortium.* Ballard was too obsessed with finding Wade to even notice, or, perhaps, *care,* that he was heading for a fall, clear down to the level of the 'lower classes' he'd despised for so long.

But he wasn't prepared to rest on the word of some hick lawman that they couldn't find the fugitive Wade. He couldn't sit still in his mansion in Ballard County, not knowing. So he organized his own posse and set out to scour all the country within a hundred miles of the site of the train wreck, investigating every so-called sighting of the escaped killer, no matter how dubious it sounded.

His expenditure was already approaching the amount of the bounty he had placed on Wade's head, but in this case, money was of no consequence to him.

The posse was still heading north, the gross, but hard-muscled figure of Ballard in the lead on his long-striding black Arab steed, when, one sundown, he led them into Handsome. Here they were forced to face the fact that their weary, hard-ridden mounts needed to be re-shod, in a few cases, have entire sets of shoes replaced. They needed grain, too, and fresh hay, attention to their coats. He resented the delay, made the blacksmith a preposterous offer to get the posse on the road again by sundown the next day, even though the shoes had yet to be forged and sized. No one could blame the blacksmith for being dazzled by the offer, and at least trying to make the deadline that would make him rich . . .

It was while Ballard was having supper in the town's best hotel — a dump by the rich man's standards — that Amy's wire finally reached him, having been forwarded from the town of Ballard and other places it was known his posse would pass through, until it finally caught up with him here in Handsome.

Only three of the ten posse horses had been shod so far, one his Arab. The 'smith was working overtime but Ballard was too impatient to wait for all the shoes to be made, and fitted, knowing from what he had seen that the process would cause a long delay. He simply couldn't sit on news like this!

So, he pushed away the plate of tasteless food he had been toying with when the message arrived, and selected two of his fastest and deadliest gun-slingers: Frisco-John Hawkins and Marsh Cadell, interrupting their meal peremptorily.

'Get your gear — we're riding for Wildspot.'

'Tonight?' asked Cadell, mouth full of potatoes and steak.

'*Now!*'

Ballard swung away from the table,

his napkin still trailing from his belt, and with a pounding stride, made for the door, yelling over his shoulder, 'Right this goddamn minute!'

Luckily the dining room door was open or he would have walked straight through it.

Before leaving, Ballard made a bad mistake: the remainder of his men, seven dirty, weary riders, who had endured the hardships of a mobile posse chase and Ballard's insults for a share in the big bounty, were told curtly that their services would no longer be required.

'Head back home and your normal jobs — you'll be paid a good daily rate for your time so far.'

'Daily rate!' exclaimed one middle-aged man, Jim Ryker, father of three. 'Judas priest, that'll be nowhere near the share you promised!'

'That was a different deal — I know where to find Wade now and I'll only need two men with me. Stay overnight if you want and I'll pay your bills, have a good time — or a reasonably good time, but start back to Ballard first thing in the morning. You don't like the deal, consider yourselves fired — as of now.'

Not even a 'thank you' for the hard work done . . . And Jim Ryker wasn't the only one riled. Ballard didn't realize it, but he had just made seven more enemies — not gunmen or killers, but hard-working range men, some with families, who had been willing to take some chances and put up with hard times for a thousand dollar share in the bounty.

But these were the men who could make more trouble for him than he had ever dreamed of.

★   ★   ★

Because she hadn't had any word from Ballard, Amy Stokes thought that, somehow, her wire had gone astray. Or that he had simply ignored her message — no doubt he received dozens, people 'seeing' the fugitive wherever they looked — with a big sign on his hat saying *I'm worth $10,000!* The bounty was the incentive, not any thoughts of 'good citizenship' or 'civic duty' or even truth. It was quite possible her wire had been seen in this light, though she had hoped she had made it sound genuine by giving Clinton's name. But deep down, all along, she had been afraid this might happen — and knew that left her only one solution now.

She would get a gun and go after Clinton herself.

★ ★ ★

Tom Pardoe had his worries. He was certain sure Ballard and his men would be on their way to Wildspot after Amy's wire. They would come a'thundering, ready to walk all over the town if what he'd heard about Julius Ballard was true.

He had no deputies, though could likely call on a couple of reliable townsmen in a pinch — but he didn't want to expose his friends to the kind of violence Ballard would bring with him. The man might have no particular sway up here, but he had so many contacts in high places that any problems he encountered after his actions could be soon fixed.

Tom didn't know yet how Ballard's associates were banding together to oust him from his high perch, seizing the chance while it was there.

Ballard didn't know it yet, either —

The sheriff was coming out of the office on to the landing where a carpenter was fixing the broken railing. Packing tobacco into his inevitable pipe bowl, and reaching for a vesta in his shirt pocket. Pardoe saw a rider going fast along Main, swinging to the south-east. He squinted, said to the carpenter: 'Who's that in such a damn hurry?'

The young carpenter shaded his eyes and said, 'Looks like that woman that seems to have her knife into Vern Clinton.'

'Amy Stokes?'

The carpenter shrugged. 'If that's her name.' He went back to chiselling a mortice in the new upright post.

Pardoe frowned, then slipped his pipe into his pocket, grabbed his hat and jammed it on. He kicked some of the carpenter's scattered tools in his hurry to get down the steps.

'That's OK, Sheriff, don't worry about it. I've got an oilstone to sharpen them three chisel blades that just got chipped. And I can pick up all them scattered nails in my lunch break . . . long as I don't take time to eat.'

Pardoe ignored him and hurried down to the livery where he called loud and urgently for the hostler.

Gene Tomkins came out of a stall, a bridle in his hands. 'The hell's all the shoutin', Tom? Judas priest, place is like One-tooth Sadie's Sin Parlour on pay day, this mornin'! Everyone comin' in, shoutin' for this, that or the other — wantin' everythin' immediately, if not sooner.'

Pardoe held up a hand, cut in

sharply. 'Amy Stokes been in?'

Tomkins chomped his toothless jaws a little, then nodded curtly. 'Yeah, just collected her hoss.'

'Say where she was goin'?'

Tomkins sighed. 'Not exactly — she said she had to meet someone at Turkey Ford an' asked me the quickest way to get to Cross Iron from there.'

Pardoe pursed his lips, frowning. 'Shoot! Saddle my hoss, Gene! And I mean *pronto*!'

'Why should you be any different!' Tomkins shouted for the stable boy. 'Cascara! Git the sheriff's hoss saddled. He's in a bigger hurry than the damn Blight brothers were . . . '

Pardoe snapped his head up. 'What the hell were those lazy sonuvers in such a hurry for?'

'I dunno. They headed out in the same direction as — Hey! you s'pose that gal was meetin' them at Turkey Ford?'

That was *exactly* what Pardoe thought. 'Hurry up with my mount!' he snapped.

He paced back and forth: The Blight

brothers — into every kind of shady deal that would make them a dollar. Cunning and sneaky as trash-pit rats, they would do anything for a fast buck. *Could she have hired them to go after Clinton, knowing she would be suspect if anything happened to him . . . ?*

'No, by God!' he murmured half-aloud, startling the young black boy saddling his horse for him. The Blights had been known to deal in guns at all levels and the fact was Amy Stokes' carbine was locked away in his gun cupboard. But they would want their trading done outside of town.

And that would suit Amy: Pardoe was the last person she'd want to know she was interested in buying a firearm.

★   ★   ★

The Blights didn't know specifically why she wanted a gun. But they knew that, if she was buying from them, then she didn't want anyone else to know about it.

So, being the kind of sharp traders they were, Randy and Chuck Blight figured they could practically name their own price — or as much as the market would bear. They had told her to bring cash — 'a goodly amount, ma'am,' Randy had said with a smile. He was the best looking of the two and had an easy way with women. Some women, anyway.

She took all the money she had: slightly more than two hundred dollars — and was surprised when they offered her a Winchester rifle with the full-size twenty-eight inch barrel for exactly that amount — almost as if they knew her limit.

'I don't want a full-size rifle — and I'm darn sure I could buy one for much less than that.'

Randy gave her his warmest smile. 'Well, you just go right ahead, ma'am — we ain't forcin' you to pay our price.'

They knew she had to deal with them!

'We'll throw in a box of shells,'

Chuck said, a much plainer-looking Blight and with a hard face and shifty eyes.

Randy adjusted his neckerchief and looked Amy straight in the eye, spoke gently, half-smiling. 'Er — mebbe we could come to some other kinda arrangement — so you mightn't have to spend any money at all — but you'd still have the gun.'

Her face tightened, as did her grip on the reins of her chestnut gelding. 'All right — I'll pay you the two hundred.'

Randy looked mildly disappointed: it wasn't often that his charm didn't work. He glanced at his brother and shrugged.

'Mebbe she could pay — and still make other arrangements,' Chuck suggested, tongue running around his rubbery lower lip lasciviously. 'I got a suggestion . . .'

'Now there's an idea!' Randy agreed enthusiastically. 'I reckon we could be generous and knock somethin' off the price — a few dollars, mebbe — would all depend on you, ma'am. You know what I mean?'

'I know *exactly* what you mean!' Amy said sharply, wrenched the reins, and raked with her heels: this was one time she wished she was wearing spurs! But the gelding responded quickly, jumping across the front of the Blights' mounts, startling them, causing them to rear up and snort and whinny. The chestnut veered away sharply. Amy wasn't prepared for it, snatched at the saddlehorn, sliding to one side. By then Chuck had jumped his big dappled workhorse forward. It rammed the chestnut and the gelding whinnied as it went down. Amy was thrown from the saddle and Randy, laughing, spurred forward, leaned out and scooped her up with one arm.

She fought and kicked and struggled, clawing at his face, and he had to turn her loose. She hit the ground awkwardly and rolled over in the dust. Chuck was out of the saddle on the instant, grabbing her by the hair and heaving her to her feet.

She gave a cry, reaching up with her hands to take some of the strain off her hair. Chuck shook her hard enough to make her teeth rattle, then backhanded her twice across the face. Randy hurriedly dismounted, feeling his face stinging from where her nails had gouged the flesh. Cursing, he reached for her blouse, hand closing brutally over her breast. She screamed.

And then Pardoe came galloping across the ford, muddy water spraying in sparkling silver droplets as he palmed up his Colt, yelling to the Blights.

'Leave her go, you sons of bitches!'

Worked-up in more ways than one, the Blights saw only a medium-sized rider, crouched low in the saddle, with a sixgun in one hand, his mount's mane streaming across his face Leaning forward like that, his star wasn't visible. The Blights merely saw someone riding in to shut down their idea of 'fun'.

'Chuck?' Randy called breathlessly as Amy's blouse tore and exposed one of her white breasts.

Chuck's eyes popped and he yelled, 'Get him!' not caring who the intruder was, reaching for his sixgun.

Then Pardoe's Colt roared and Chuck spun around, clutching at a place high on his chest. He dropped to one knee, still able to bring up his Colt. Pardoe twisted in his crouched position, swinging his smoking gun toward Randy. The good-looking Blight — not so handsome now with his lips drawn back into a snarl — held his gun in both hands and triggered two shots. At the same moment, the sheriff fired and Randy crashed backwards, no longer good-looking, his face only a mess of blood and torn flesh and splintered bone.

Chuck roared to his feet, staggering, blood on his chest, weaving as he fired. Pardoe was driven from the saddle. He hit hard, rolled on to his belly and propped his elbows into the ground, shooting. Chuck staggered, his legs starting to collapse. Pardoe shot him again. Chuck tilted to one side, hit the ground and lay with wide, staring eyes, the lustre fading quickly.

Shaking, and instinctively tucking her torn blouse in to cover her embarrassment, Amy ran to kneel by Pardoe, trying to lift him to a half-sitting position.

'Sheriff! Sheriff! — I-I'm so dreadfully sorry! This is all my fault . . . '

'Makes no — nevermind — now, missy . . . ' he gasped.

His head slumped on to his chest and she felt warm blood trickle across her hand.

11

Lawman

She didn't know how long she had been sitting there, numbed, guilty, with Pardoe's bloody body across her bent legs.

But suddenly, she became aware of another presence, turned her head slowly — and jumped when a man with a rifle stepped out of some trees on this side of the ford.

'So this is what all the shooting was about?' Vern Clinton said, hurrying forward to kneel beside her, looking at Pardoe. 'Is he still alive?'

'I-I'm — not sure — I — caught him as he fell and I was so shocked . . . I haven't checked for a pulse yet . . . '

'Goddamnit, woman, let me get a look at him.'

Clinton was rough with her but he

made sure he was between her and the rifle he had placed on the ground at all times. 'He's still breathing — tough old codger.'

'I don't think I could've lifted him across his horse, anyway.'

'Those other two dead?'

'Yes — The sheriff shot them. They were — roughing me up.'

'Doesn't show much,' he told her unsympathetically, taking off his neckerchief and wiping blood away from the wound in Pardoe's lower chest. 'With a bit of luck, the bullet's missed anything vital. Cracked some ribs, likely when he fell off his horse. We'll try to stop the bleeding and get him to the sawbones . . . Well, come on! Find some rags to rip up for bandages — and stay away from those guns lying near those dead men.'

Suddenly her eyes blazed, as his terse tone and words jarred her out of her shock. 'Who're you ordering about?'

'You! Now for Chris'sake get a move on. You can take time to be offended or whatever you like after we get Pardoe into town.'

She swallowed, face reddening, and then she took hold of herself and went to her saddle-bags, bringing out a fresh, though crumpled white blouse. She went behind a bush, took off the torn pale green blouse and buttoned on the other. She flung the torn garment in Clinton's direction.

'Tear it into strips!' he snapped. 'I'm keeping pressure on this neckerchief I've wadded over the wound. Hurry up so we can bind it in place . . . '

'God, I wish I'd shot you the first time I saw you.'

'Just get moving.'

When she brought the green bandage strips and had tied them over the wadded neckerchief, he stood up and went to the dead men.

They were strangers to him. He took their sixguns and rifles, and flung them into the creek, off the edge of the ford where the water was deeper. He picked up the big rifle the Blights had tried to sell Amy, worked the lever so the cartridges were ejected, glittering in the sunlight. He recovered them and dropped them into his pocket.

She watched him, her features tight, starting to show a little bruising from Randy's and Chuck's rough handling. 'I was buying that to finish the job I started.'

He said nothing, rammed the unloaded weapon through his bedroll straps behind the cantle. He took his work rope and, with her help, wound a dozen coils firmly around Pardoe's torso to help support his damaged ribs. He used the remainder of the rope to tie the sheriff in the saddle.

'We'll keep him between us, ride in close and hold him as steady as we can.'

She gave him a half-smirk. 'Making sure my hands are occupied, are you?'

'He's an old man, tough as sun-dried leather, but still old. He's gonna have to fight hard to pull through. Might not even make it to town.'

'Would it be better if we stayed here

and — let him die in peace instead of giving him a rough ride?'

His look was blistering. 'He's not dead yet . . . '

They hadn't ridden far when they heard a shout and a clatter of fast-approaching hoofs.

Amy gasped once again at the speed Clinton's Colt appeared in his right hand as he hipped slightly in the saddle, but kept his left hand steadying the wounded sheriff.

Yuma Hardy slowed his mount and rode alongside Clinton and Amy. He glanced at the girl and then Pardoe.

'Blue said when you an' him were fellin' some trees you heard shootin' and come to check it out. Who shot Tom?'

Clinton glanced at Amy and she told Yuma it was the Blight brothers, gesturing to the sprawled dead men.

'Well, they ain't no loss — I see they had a mite more in mind than just sellin' you a gun, miss.'

She flushed a little and the bruising stood out more plainly. 'The sheriff came in time but — I'm afraid he's badly wounded.'

'Can you bury the Blights or cover 'em with rocks or something, Yuma?' Clinton asked. 'Don't want to delay getting Tom into town.'

Yuma nodded, reining aside, looking at the girl. 'Things all right between you two now?'

They both said an emphatic No! simultaneously.

'Mebbe I better fetch Blue. He can bury the Blights and I'll ride in with you . . . '

'Oh, don't be concerned for him!' Amy said disdainfully, glaring. 'I don't have a gun — at the moment.'

Yuma arched querying eyebrows at Clinton who simply shrugged. Then he pulled his horse back a little more and touched a hand to his hatbrim.

'Hope Tom makes it — and you two.'

'What did he mean?' queried the girl as Yuma rode off. 'And you two . . . ?'

'Guess he doesn't want us to kill each other.'

She straightened a little, losing her grip slightly.

'Watch it, dammit!'

Her mouth tightened as she threw him a bleak look.

'He won't have to worry about us killing 'each other' — I'm, just going to kill you sooner or later — preferably sooner!'

Clinton smiled crookedly, sardonically. 'I can live with that.'

'Oh! You — you — smartmouth! If I didn't have to steady Sheriff Pardoe . . . '

'Lucky me.'

They didn't exchange another word until they reached the doctor's in Wildspot.

★ ★ ★

After a cursory examination of the lawman, Doctor Burns said, 'Well, I don't think the bullet's done a lot of damage. Actually, it's not in there now. Skidded round one of those cracked ribs and burst out. His age is against

198

him: blood loss and falling as well as the gunshot wound — quite a shock to the system for a man his age . . . '

The medic was moving about as he spoke, getting a tin dish of water and clouding it with some added disinfectant. He rolled up his sleeves and began to wash his hands. He glanced at the girl.

'I could use some help, young lady. My wife's not here today, you have a strong stomach?'

She smiled and Clinton, despite himself, saw how her begrimed and bruised face lit up with warmth. 'I'm not a trained nurse, doctor, but I tended my invalid mother for almost five years before she — succumbed.'

He smiled in return, noting the sadness that had edged her voice. 'Then, between us, we ought to be able to pull our lawman through. You could help me get him on to my operating table, Mr Clinton, and then — perhaps you could find him some clean clothes for him, or long underwear: he has living quarters behind the law office.'

'I'll look, Doc — Good luck.'

'Good man, that Clinton,' Burns remarked as he left. The girl said nothing, her face in straight lines. 'Over the years, I've learned to read people fairly well, my dear — and take my word for it, he's a good man. Has a sense of honour. 'Code' they like to call it here . . . The kind who, if he gives his word, will stand by it.'

'You could be wrong at least some of the time, doctor,' was all Amy said and he nodded slowly.

'Always that chance,' he agreed quietly.

★ ★ ★

As Clinton stepped back into Pardoe's office, some clothing jammed into an old pillowcase, he saw a man standing there, with some kind of paper in his hand.

'Oh — I was looking for the sheriff.'

'He's been wounded — pretty badly. Doc's tending him now.'

'Oh, my.' The man looked worriedly at the yellow form he held. 'I'm Hank Rollins, the telegraph agent. There's this wire from the Rangers in Dallas. Seems they've sent the same message to a lot of sheriffs . . . '

He turned the paper and Clinton set down the bundle and read the message:

To all Peace Officers in the Sovereign State of Texas: Detain and/or arrest one Julius Ballard, of Ballard County. Wanted for perjury, fraud and other crimes. Ranger sent on request. Joplin, Chief Officer, Dallas Ranger H.Q.

'Ballard's here?' Clinton asked sharply.

'Dunno. Sounds like he's expected. What should I do with the wire?'

'I'm going back to the doctor's now — I'll show it to Pardoe if he's conscious — Doc might have some suggestion.'

Rollins looked dubious. 'It's addressed to the sheriff — I-I ought give it to him myself. I really shouldn't've shown it to you.'

Clinton picked up the pillowcase of clothing impatiently. 'Then bring it along.'

Doc Burns pursed his lips after reading the message. 'He's conscious, but not too lucid yet: you hand him the wire and leave it with him, Hank. You'll have done your job then.'

Rollins was glad to have someone make the decision for him, went with the medic into Pardoe's room and left shortly after, not so worried-looking.

Amy came in and stopped when she saw Clinton.

'How is he?'

'Surprisingly well,' she told him evenly. 'The doctor is very pleased — but worried there may be a relapse.'

Clinton nodded and started for the door. Then Burns poked his head around the door of Pardoe's room. 'Before you go, Mr Clinton . . . '

When he entered the room, Clinton was surprised to see Pardoe half-sitting, propped up on pillows, scrawny chest with its light mat of grey hair, crisscrossed with fresh bandages. The lawman looked grey and drawn, but lifted a finger in greeting, holding the telegraph message in his other hand. His eyelids drooped.

'Seems — Ballard got — the gal's — wire.' His voice was croaky and shaky.

'Not too much talking, Tom,' admonished the doctor.

'Seems like it,' Clinton replied to Pardoe. 'You got a deputy?'

Pardoe shook his head carefully. 'Never needed one. How you feel — about takin' — a-a deputy's oath?'

Clinton stiffened. 'Me? I'm a wanted fugitive.'

'I — dunno that. I got no dodger on — a — Vern Clinton.' Pardoe said breathlessly, and the doctor moved in, took one wrist and checked his pulse.

'Tom, you shouldn't . . . ' Burns broke off as he looked quickly at Clinton. He half-smiled. 'What do you think about taking that oath and becoming a lawman, be it only temporarily . . . ?'

'Well, like I said, I . . . ' Clinton stopped, frowned and then a very slight smile touched his lips and Doctor Burns chuckled.

'Thought you might see a nice touch of irony in such a move. Having the power to arrest the man who has made your life hell for the past six or seven years . . . '

'Would feel kinda good.'

* * *

Hank Rollins sat at his desk, just signing-off a message with his rapid tap-tappety-tap call sign. The narrow doorway of the office was darkened briefly and then Vern Clinton entered. Rollins sat up straight in his chair.

'The — sheriff — he OK?' Clinton nodded. 'I-I was wonderin' if I did the right thing, showin' you that message — when it was addressed to Tom, I mean.'

'It was addressed to *All Lawmen*.' Clinton stepped closer and allowed

Rollins to see the star pinned to Clinton's shirt pocket. The man's jaw dropped. 'I'm deputy while the sheriff's recovering — Judge Tillyer just swore me in.'

Hank Rollins looked relieved as well as surprised. He wiped a hand across his sweat-beaded forehead. 'Then, I pass on to you any more messages about Ballard that come in?'

'That's official, Hank.' The agent couldn't help smiling and sagging in his chair: his job was safe. 'Anything else for me?'

'Er — no.' He rummaged through a sheaf of message forms, looked up and shook his head, saying again, 'No — er — Deputy.'

'OK. Bring me anything that comes in to do with Ballard.'

He went next door to the stage depot, asked to check the passenger lists but wasn't surprised that Ballard wasn't booked on any stages due.

He would likely ride in at the head of his own posse.

All he could do was wait.

He decided to take a walk around the town, let folk see the badge, catch their reactions. He smiled, knowing that most townsfolk would throw a double fit when they realized they had a gunslinger for a lawman.

He wondered how Amy Stokes would take it . . . If she persisted in her attempts at killing him now, she would be killing a duly-sworn lawman.

That meant big trouble if she was successful.

12

Enemies

Clinton felt out of his depth. And yet, somehow eager to make a good fist of his new job.

He had sent word to Yuma and Blue and the buck-toothed kid who conveyed the message brought back a note from Yuma.

Congratulations to the new lawman. Your old friend Bracken's men have been spotted watching The Bench lately. Take care — Luke has a looooong memory and a delicate ego.

That disturbed Clinton some: he had known Bracken would do something to square with him after the fist fight, but he didn't want him to take out his revenge on Yuma or Blue.

At the same time, he couldn't very well leave town when Ballard was expected at any time. So he checked with Pardoe who told him there was an emergency account available to pay for extra temporary deputies in time of trouble and that could be used to hire a couple of men to watch the three trails into Wildspot. So that was what Clinton did, hired three men lounging around the saloon.

'We think he'll be leading a posse so watch for a good-sized dust cloud or a bunch of riders — no idea how many. But get word to me, pronto.'

They were cowboys, unemployed right now, and knew the country and the best vantage points.

The next morning he was visiting Pardoe who was making slow but good progress, though the doctor was strict about short visiting times. Clinton was just leaving when one of the men he had watching the trails, came hurrying into the doctor's.

'Deputy! There's a good-size dust cloud on the trail comin' in from the far side of Calico Mountain. You know, where Yuma's settin'-up . . . ?'

'Right, Frank — I'll go check. Want to earn a couple more bucks by siding me . . . ?'

Frank, a stubbled, hard-looking cowpoke, held up both hands. 'No, sir! You're the kind attracts gunplay, you don't mind me sayin', Deputy — I'll watch for you, but I ain't no good with guns.'

He left and as Clinton started after him, Amy came out of Pardoe's room with a cloth covered bedpan and went out another door. The doctor crossed quickly to Clinton's side.

'Vern, that man, Frank Borden, used to work for Bracken. One of his hardcases, beating-up nesters and so on.'

'Obliged, Doc.' Clinton nodded and went out.

He rode out of town towards Calico Mountain ten minutes later, using his mount hard, but scanning the country he rode through with every stride it took.

He made his way up the lower slopes of Calico Mountain, glimpsing Yuma's Flying Y in three places as he followed the winding trail. His mount was part quarter-horse, stocky and tough, suited to rough country like this, though not so good for speed, but endurance came easy to it.

He knew where Frank Borden had been setting-up to watch the trail over the rise, and veered towards the place. He had to admit that he hadn't expected Ballard to approach from this angle — if, indeed, it was Ballard's posse that had been seen — but no one knew just where the man was so it was more than possible. And it wasn't likely there would be another posse in that area just now.

In fact, there didn't seem to be any posse at all.

He had his field glasses in his hands, sitting his horse on an outcrop, ready to scan the expected dust cloud. But there was no dust at all, not even a thin haze, lifted by the gentle breeze that slid down from the slopes.

Doc's warning about Frank Borden's past association with Bracken could be more timely than anyone had figured . . .

He realized this just too late. A heavy rifle crashed and his big horse snorted, jerked its head and reared up, pawing the air, blood spurting from just above the left eye. He had held the mount in close against a large boulder rising beside him and he was thrown heavily against it now, losing his grip on the reins, feet sliding out of the stirrups. He heard the field glasses splinter against the rock and then there was an explosion in his head and he passed out so quickly, he didn't even have the sensation of falling.

The echoes of the gunfire rebounded around the hills fading swiftly. Gunsmoke drifted down from the rocks above and the birds that had been frightened into flight whirled and squawked against the hot blue sky.

Then a man stood up amongst the

pile of rocks clinging to a steep part of the slope, levering another shell into the rifle's breech. He stepped out, moving stiffly, placing his feet carefully, the bandages around his head showing beneath his battered hat. One eye was swollen but not entirely closed, his mouth a mangled piece of raw meat and the nose hammered into something like a piece of clay after a child had finished playing with it.

Luke Bracken spat and tried to grin with his battered mouth as he plodded down the slope to where Clinton lay, partly jammed behind the dead horse. He came on, steps slow and deliberate, boots thudding sometimes on loose rocks. He balanced carefully until he felt the rock firm and then slid his foot off on to more solid ground: a man suffering from his injuries . . .

He stopped about ten feet from Clinton who was stirring slowly, blood streaking his face, left arm caught beneath his body. His eyes flickered open as Bracken spoke.

'Din' think I'd let a piece of tin scare me off squarin' with you, did you, gunslinger? Huh? You hear? It don't scare me none that you're some kinda lawman. You'll bleed just as much as when you was a plain pain-in-the-ass cowpoke workin' for Yuma. An' ain't he in for a surprise when he finds out he's no longer got his gunslinger sidekick to get him outta trouble!' He leaned forward from the waist. 'Whatsa matter, big man? Cat got your tongue? Ah, don't matter. I don't wanta hear anythin' outta you — 'cept your scream when I shoot you in the belly' He raised the rifle and sighted down the barrel with his good eye, finger loosely curled around the trigger.

''Course you know who'll get the blame for this, don't you . . . ? That feisty bitch who wants to kill you for downin' her old man. Gonna be perfect, ain't it?'

'I don't think so!'

Bracken stiffened fleetingly and swung from the hips, the rifle coming around and shooting towards the sound of the voice. Another rifle fired simultaneously and there was a clapping, rolling mix of the double shot resounding across Calico Mountain.

Bracken was blown backwards, his big gun falling from his grip. His body struck some scree and it slid from under, taking him with it as it flooded down the slope and over a ledge with a drop of about twenty feet on to rocks.

The sound when his body struck came clearly to the ledge where Clinton lay, struggling to get free, looking at his saviour standing on a flat rock with a smoking rifle.

It was a very whitefaced Amy Stokes.

★   ★   ★

His fall against the big boulder had split open the nearly-healed scar of his scalp wound and that side of his face was streaked with blood. He wrenched off his neckerchief and held it over the wound, blinking at the girl who hadn't moved in all the time it had taken him to free himself from behind the dead horse.

She held the rifle in both hands, at arms' length, down in front of her, just staring at him, stunned.

He held the kerchief in his left hand, awkwardly, his scalp wound being on the right side of his head. But he wanted his right hand close to his gun butt until he saw what she was going to do next.

'Were you aiming at me or him?' he asked, not being deliberately provocative, but trying to jar her out of whatever condition she was in right now.

A faint frown appeared between her eyes and they blinked, and she turned them directly on him, seeing him clearly for the first time since the shooting, he figured.

'What did you say?'

'I said good shooting — you saved my neck — even if it wasn't your intention.'

The small jaw squared and thrust slightly forward. The knuckles whitened around the rifle. 'I should've expected that would be the kind of thanks I'd get!'

He relaxed some, ashamed he was needling her. 'I'm sorry, Amy. Bit of reaction. I thought I was a goner. Where'd you come from . . . ?' Then he answered his own question. 'Sure — you passed through the room at Doc's and heard Borden tell me he'd spotted Ballard's posse. You decided to take advantage of it, get me out of sight of town and — Where'd you get the gun?'

She stared down at it for a long moment. 'Did you know Doc Burns has a son who is a crack shot? He won this at some turkey shoot a few years ago and Doc kept it on the wall after his son joined the army . . . '

'Easier to get hold of than through the Blight brothers.'

'Yes! And I intended to shoot you with it.'

'Well, I'm glad your aim was off and you hit Bracken instead. Or was it intentional?'

'I-I've never shot at anyone before. Oh, I know I gave that impression, but I — ' He watched her gulp down a deep breath and the tears ran down her face, tracking through the film of dust. He heard her efforts to stifle a sob. 'I — thought it'd be so — easy to shoot you! I've hated you all those years since you killed Rapido! I-I wanted so badly to — kill you — but Ma was ailing and I-I couldn't leave — until she — passed on and then I set out to look for you.'

He felt uncomfortable and spoke quietly. 'Well, you sure muffed your chance today — I'm glad to say.'

'Maybe I'll have — another chance,' she said and suddenly she shouted, '*Draw!*'

She never even saw his gun leave leather and then it was obscured by the powder-smoke and she collapsed, the rifle falling over the edge of the flat rock, one of her arms hanging limply . . .

Clinton felt his blood pounding. 'God almighty! You crazy damn fool! Putting me to the test like that! I-I could've killed you — Judas, mebbe I have!'

He climbed up to her but she was alive, though shaking and pale. She twisted away from him and retched. He took a clean kerchief from his pocket and handed it to her silently. *She was really shaken by what she had done.*

He helped her to where she had tethered her horse and she rinsed her mouth out with canteen water. He felt her still shaking as he held her arm.

'I — that was — stupid of me, wasn't it?'

'Damn right . . . lucky I shot to one side. Only just had time . . . '

'Was that — how you reacted when Rapido shouted 'draw'?' His jaw was tight and he nodded jerkily. 'I — have been reading some of the doctor's medical books — especially on head wounds, depressed head wounds — I knew something was wrong with

Rapido on that last visit to us — Ma was deteriorating and out of her head with the pain — It upset him terribly. He crashed out of the house in the middle of the night and — and I never saw him again. I couldn't believe he had turned from the loving, warm and funny father I knew into some kind of — madman.'

She paused, gasping for breath in her emotion. 'I blamed you, and when I heard some of Jinglebob's versions I was sure you'd provoked him, taking advantage of his condition so you could claim the title of 'fastest gun' ... I convinced myself that was how it happened. After all you were serving time for having provoked that Ballard boy.'

He was too stunned by her admissions to say much. 'What changed your mind? That's if you have changed it ...'

She made a small movement of her lips that might have been a very fleeting smile. 'I-I don't know. But, I'll admit — I don't want to kill you any more

— I-I don't want to kill anyone — ever again!'

She broke down this time, sobbing terribly. He stood there, statue-stiff, not knowing what to do.

Then she threw her arms about him, a distraught human being seeking comfort wherever it was available. She sobbed against his chest and he felt the warm tears soaking through his shirt front. After a while he put his arms about her lightly and held her until she apparently couldn't cry any more. He lowered her to the rock.

'Rest here — I'll go find Bracken's horse and then head back to town — There might've been a real sighting of Ballard by now.'

She said nothing, didn't even lift her head, just sat there hugging her knees. She avoided looking at him, in a world of her own — and suffering in some way, he knew.

He climbed back up the slope, hearing Bracken's mount whinny from behind a stand of boulders.

Doc Burns gave Clinton's scalp wound some cursory treatment, washed with disinfectant, smeared with a healing pomade.

Amy, acting as his nurse, cleared away the medic's things while Clinton told about the run-in with Bracken.

'That man Borden lied to you about having seen the dust of many riders approaching and Bracken waited to ambush you — is that what happened?'

'That's it, Doc. If you hadn't warned me about Borden I might not have been so alert — even so, you could've flattened me with a powder-puff when Amy there shot Bracken.'

She made a small noise and they glanced at her, saw the sallow colour of her face and Clinton knew he had made a mistake, reminding her — though he would have thought she wouldn't need any reminding about that afternoon.

'Sorry, Amy, but I owe you my life and I want folk to know about it.'

'I-I'd rather they didn't.'

'I'm sure Mr Clinton will respect your wishes, Amy,' Doc Burns said, looking sternly at Clinton.

'Yeah — sure. Folk'll think I shot it out with Bracken, anyway. Better report to Pardoe.'

'He's sleeping — come back later.'

As the doctor held the door open for him, Clinton nodded at Amy but she was busying herself cleaning up. As he passed Burns he said in a low voice,

'Keep an eye on her, Doc. She's not as tough as she made out — and killing a man for the first time ain't easy to live with for a while.'

'I doubt that girl will ever find it easy to live with.'

Walking back to the law office, people on the boardwalks staring at him — they had seen him bring in the body of Luke Bracken — he saw Hank Rollins standing outside the telegraph office, gesturing for him to come across.

'More wires, Hank?' Clinton asked when he was inside and wondered why

Rollins closed the street door.

'Er, not exactly. You see, when things are kinda — slow — we sometimes call each other up and have what we call a 'Crow Session' . . . other telegraphists an' me, I mean. You ever see a bunch of crows all lined-up or even in a circle, cawin' fit to drive you loco while they gossiped?'

'Lot of times.'

'Yeah — well, we exchange a bit of news and this 'n' that — '

'Gossip — rumours?'

Hank heaved a sigh. 'Yeah, OK — but lots of times it's real news. Like — this feller Ballard.'

Clinton felt himself tighten.

'Seems he's got lotsa things goin': big cattle ranch, of course, but backin' railroads, got interest in some silver or gold mines . . . '

'Yeah, he's a big noise, Hank. What of it?'

'Well — seems he's a bossy type, made enemies of everyone he deals with — but he makes 'em money so they put up with it — 'cept after that feller that killed his son — '

'Me.'

'Er — yeah. After you escaped, he let everything slide, only wanted to run you down and string you up or somethin'. His partners couldn't even contact him lots of times to sign important papers and they lost money on contracts and buyin' cattle, cheaper steel for train tracks — all 'cause they couldn't get his OK.'

'You got all this from other telegraph operators?'

'Oh, sure. You'd be surprised what passes through our keys. Why I could tell you some things about the Governor himself — '

'Stick to Ballard.'

'OK — Well, cuttin' a long story short, he's neglected his business in the hunt for you, so bad, the other consortium members — he runs what he calls the Lone Star Consortium — well, they've voted him out.'

Clinton frowned. 'Out? Of what?'

'The consortium! He's used their money tryin' to find you and for other things he oughta pay for himself. So they've made a vote of no confidence — and have started legal action agin him for fraud.'

Clinton let it sink in, asked a few more questions to be clarified and then smiled, clapping Rollins on the arm.

'You're a damn old gossip, Hank! Thank the Good Lord! Now you may not know what's happened to me the last seven years since I had that gunfight with Gavin Ballard . . . '

'Yeah, I know. We've all heard.'

Clinton shook his head. 'You've heard, but you don't know, Hank. Nobody does unless they've been on that goddamn rockpile and chain-gang — ' He stopped to draw a deep breath. 'No matter — it's over now. Obliged for you telling me. Don't suppose you know what Ballard did to perjure himself?'

Hank grinned, for the first time looking less than worried. 'You mean why you gotta hold him for the Rangers and US Marshals, perjury comin' under federal law . . . '

Clinton looked at him in surprise. 'You are a mighty knowledgeable man, it seems, Hank.'

Rollins looked pleased. 'Yeah, well that come through on another crow session: seems Ballard did the dirty on some of his posse, down in Handsome. Fired 'em, refused to pay 'em what he promised. So feller named Jim Ryker went to the Rangers and told 'em he and several others had been bribed by Ballard himself to swear that you had provoked Gavin into the gunfight. In which case, I'd say your conviction will have to be overturned — and you can be the new sheriff of Wildspot if Tom Pardoe ain't up to it . . . '

Clinton felt light-headed. *Surely this couldn't be happening!*

But it was. There would have to be a lot of legal work done but it seemed as if he *would* be able to lead a more or less ordinary life — once he changed his name again and found some lonesome range a long way from Texas where he could live in peace . . .

Then a man from the saloon knocked on the door, and when admitted said,

'Feller about the size of a seven-passenger stage is in the saloon askin' about you, Mr Clinton.'

'Give his name?'

'Yessir — Julius Ballard.'

'He alone?'

The man hesitated. 'I'm — not sure — There's two other fellers in the bar with the same kinda dust on their clothes and hats and faces as Ballard — Never spoke to him but I kinda got the impression they mighta come in together and split up . . . '

Clinton gave the man a silver dollar. 'Don't say you found me. I'll be along . . . '

The man went out, but as he was closing the door, paused long enough to see Clinton take out his sixgun and check the cylinder loads.

He entered the saloon by a side door, immediately picked out Ballard seated at a corner table, alone, a bottle of whiskey before him. As he watched, Clinton saw him mop his face and then pour himself a drink, slopping it a little.

The big man was tense.

Clinton glanced quickly at the bar before entering properly and easing the door closed behind him.

He knew Frisco-John and the man a little along from him, making out he wasn't with Frisco, had to be Marsh Cadell. He had seen him once in a gun-fight in one of the narrow streets behind the Alamo in San Antone. He was pretty fast, but pulled a hide-away gun from his belt at the middle of his back and nailed his opponent with it first before finishing him with the sixgun. *Sneaky type, and deadly.*

Frisco-John was *fast,* conventional, though it was said he had nailed a couple of men he claimed to have out-drawn by shooting first and then challenging . . .

He stepped up to Ballard's table and as his shadow fell across the big man's drink, Ballard glanced up.

His eyes were already big in the large face, reddened from long riding, but they opened wide now. He spilled his whiskey, groped for his kerchief and mopped his face quickly. He was unable to keep from throwing a glance down the smoke-hazed room to his two gunslingers at the bar. They gave no sign they had seen Clinton — but he knew they must have, facing the big bar mirror as they were.

'You haven't lost any weight, Ballard. But don't worry, the rockpile'll soon get it off you.'

Ballard had recovered now from his first shock and there was a tangible tension in the big room, some men muttering and pointing, sensing a gunfight. The wise ones found themselves somewhere they could quickly duck for cover when the bullets began to fly.

'My, my — What's this? A deputy's

star! You have come up in the world, Wade — or Clinton or whatever you call yourself ... You don't for one moment think that the sight of that badge will deter me from my task — ?'

'Dunno about that, Ballard, but it'll help deter you from a few other things.'

'Such as?'

Clinton knew the man was keeping him talking while his gunslingers got themselves into position and the room was very silent now, the air palpable with a rising tension ...

'I have a request from Ranger Head-quarters in Dallas to detain and-or arrest you in relation to forthcoming perjury charges and fraud — ' Clinton smiled. 'Will you hear me? All formal, even sound like a deputy sheriff, don't I?'

Ballard's eyes were narrowed now and there was no more bluff or mockery in him.

'Perjury? Fraud? Who dares bring such charges against me ... ?'

'The State of Texas, for one — your own Lone Star Consortium officers for another. You've been caught out, Ballard. You're finished — and here you were thinking it was the other way round. Right?'

Ballard was streaming sweat now and he was unable to contain himself any longer: it seemed to Clinton the man had actually been half-expecting these charges to catch up with him because of prolonged laxity in running his Consortium.

'Frisco! Marsh!'

Ballard's voice broke as he called out and heaved himself out of his chair, throwing his huge bulk on the floor.

Clinton spun, going down to one knee, seeing men scatter away from the bar, leaving Frisco-John and Cadell with blazing guns.

Clinton's gun hammered in a roaring blast, a couple of bullets sending splinters flying from the bar. Cadell stepped forward, but was hammered back by lead and jarred against the bar's edge. He slid down, trying to lift his gun for one more shot. Instead, he shot himself in the foot — but it's doubtful he felt it.

He was dead before he hit the floor.

Frisco vaulted the bar, running along behind it, half crouched. He knocked bottles off the shelves and the crash of them breaking marked his progress. He appeared at the end of the bar, eyed the swinging side door where some patrons had run out and made a dive for it, pulling his second pistol, dropping the first, empty one, transferring the loaded one deftly to his right hand.

It only took a blurred second — but that was all Clinton needed. He shot through the thin front panel of the bar. Wood slivers flew and Frisco yelled, staggered upright, shooting wild, a bullet smashing the mirror. He grabbed at the bar, trying to keep his feet, lifted his gun as Clinton stood swiftly and fired a shot as he rose. The lead took Frisco in the neck and flung him into a bottle shelf like a side of beef. He went down with a rain of bottles cascading on top of him.

Clinton spun as someone yelled, 'Watch out!' and he saw Ballard bringing up a double barrelled derringer in fat, shaking hands. Clinton fired his last shot into him.

It took the fat man in the right shoulder and he screamed like a woman as he dropped to his knees, blood spurting. Clinton reloaded swiftly before walking across and placing a boot on one fat hand reaching like a giant plump spider for the dropped derringer. Ballard looked up, face contorted in pain, eyes wild.

'I hope you'll fit through the door of the cell,' Clinton said. 'Couple you fellers give me a hand to heave this tub of lard to his feet will you?'

★   ★   ★

Amy Stokes watched Vern Clinton mount the new horse the town had presented him with — a big buckskin with a ring of black around one eye.

'The town wants you to stay,' she said. 'Tom Pardoe in particular . . . He

233

says he's thinking of retiring once he's properly on his feet.'

'Yeah, he asked me to stay, but — ' He shrugged. 'I owe Tom a lot, the town, and Yuma, too but' — He paused. 'I guess I owe you most of all.'

'My original intentions were not very — honorable . . . I-I'm still trying to come to terms with my feelings.' She gave him a steady look. 'It may take a little — time.'

'You're doing good. The Rangers've got Ballard and they tell me I'll have my name cleared and a pardon once they prosecute him. Then I'll find someplace where I can slot myself in as an ordinary rancher or cowhand or something. If I keep my own name or come back here sooner or later there's gonna be someone itching to see if I'm as fast as they say.'

She was sad but trying not to show it. 'Yes, I suppose so — Doctor Burns wants to train me as his nurse — I feel it's a worthwhile job. But where will you go?'

'Dunno yet. Likely well clear of Texas.'

'I think I'd like to stay in touch if you wouldn't mind. Just the occasional letter — but if I don't know what name you're using . . . '

'Why don't you pick one for me?'

She stiffened. 'Me? Oh, well — Clint Vernon? No, that's too close to what you use now. You should stay right away from 'Wade', I suppose. Oh, I don't know . . . '

'How about just plain ol' 'Jack Smith'? Address the letter to 'General Delivery'. I'll let you know the nearest town to where I am.'

She frowned. 'Yes, that's good, but there must be hundreds of Smiths! A letter could easily go astray.'

'Spell it with two t's — Smitth. It's odd but we'll know the letters are for us then: I'll write the name on the back so you can be sure — make it our own code.'

'We — Us — Our . . . ?' It had a touch of — permanency — about it, she thought . . .

He noticed the small uncertain frown between her eyes. Mentally, he shrugged, then settled into leather and lifted a hand in a brief, farewell wave.

'Sometime, then,' he said quietly but she didn't answer.

But as the horse turned all the way round, she waved hesitantly.

The frown had gone and he thought he saw her smile. Just a little.

THE END

Other titles in the
Linford Western Library:

OUTLAW CANYON

Jack Sheriff

Rafe and Seth Laramie were just trying to go home, but, mistakenly targeted by an angry posse, they are forced to flee a hail of bullets and hide out in the town of Greybull. There, the enigmatic Mort Sangster helps them to evade the posse. But all is not as it seems. The brothers follow Sangster to his cabin where outlaws, plotting an elaborate crime, invite them into the fold ... but what bloody battles lie ahead if they accept?

THE TANGLEWOOD DESPERADOES

Logan Winters

Once you entered Tanglewood, in Southern Colorado, you could never find your way out. A savage, broken landscape — it was the perfect place to hide from the law. No lawman ever entered it, preferring the Tanglewood to do his work for him. So when Trace Dawson and his gang rode in, they were men without hope. Crooked land-pirates had taken their land and their homes from them. Now they were planning to fight back, whatever that might involve . . .

SCAR COUNTY SHOWDOWN

Elliot Long

When town marshal Arthur Curry is gunned down from behind by killers unknown, his brother, Sam, comes to Columbus to pay his last respects and to seek vengeance. The mayor, an old friend of Sam's, believes he knows who is responsible for the murderous crime. But Sam makes his own investigations, which lead him head-first into a nightmare to which there is no easy solution. Time is ticking and there is a target on Sam's back . . .

THE SNAKE RIVER BOUNTY

Bill Shields

As a young man, Ben Hollinger hunted down and killed the outlaw gang who murdered his family. Now the marshal of a sleepy cattle town, he's forced into a gunfight with a young troublemaker, whom he kills — and his peace is shattered. Nate Thornton, the boy's father, owns the biggest ranch in the territory. The bounty he puts on Ben's head draws every local gun-hand to hunt him down. His only hope of survival lies with Cordelia — Thornton's daughter . . .

AMBUSH AT LAKOTA CROSSING

Terrell L. Bowers

Two old codgers manned Lakota Crossing; fifty miles from the nearest town. The perfect place for an ambush. Wayland Lott and his gang of killers were about to rob an army payroll at its way station, unaware that a bounty hunter was now working at the stage stop at Lakota Crossing. Jess Logan was pleased to finish out the winter there. But when the bandit gang began warring, the bounty hunter jumped straight into action — regardless of the consequences . . .